The Outsiders:
Book Two

Brandon Faircloth

Other Works by Brandon Faircloth:

Mystery

Darkness

On the Hill and Other Tales of Horror

Whimsical Leprosy

The Outsiders: Book One

You saw something you shouldn't have

One Bite at a Time

My Uncle Makes Dolls to Replace Souls in Hell

Incarnata

I'll Make My Arrows from Your Bones (coming soon)

Table of Contents

I found a coffin buried in my backyard. There was a letter inside.

<u>Part One</u>

My wife left me last winter. I'd like to say it was undeserved, but the truth was I had been slowly making the transition from social drinker to sloppy drunk for the past several years. If I ever was, I had stopped being a good husband or father the last couple of years for sure, and it's a miracle Sandra tried as long as she did before packing up our little girls and moving back to her old hometown.

After several months of self-pity and self-loathing, I began getting my shit together. I started attending group meetings, working harder at my job, and rebuilding a life for myself and the people I love. I never had any illusions of me and my wife getting back together—some things can't be unsaid or undone. But I did want to be a good father again. I wanted to gain joint custody and have a home that my kids could come and feel comfortable in—not the forced march trips I had seen with some divorced fathers who either didn't really want to see their kids or at least did very little to make a place for a child in their lives and their houses.

So I fixed up bedrooms for both of them. They came with their mother and picked out the colors for the walls and the furniture they wanted. I was excited to see them, but also for them to have a chance to see me. Sandra hugged me when they left, telling me that she was so happy I was doing so much better. And if I could keep it up, she added, she'd be happy to agree to joint custody.

This just motivated me further. Summer was coming up in a couple of months, and my hope was that I could get time with them during their break from school. So I looked up summer programs, found attractions and parks we could go to, and set about getting someone to put in a swimming pool.

We had talked about getting a swimming pool for years, but had never had the money. Surprisingly, working hard and not pissing away large chunks of money on booze allowed me to save up enough for a good down payment on the pool fairly quickly. By May I had workers out in my back yard with a backhoe. It was a Saturday, and I was watching them with interest and satisfaction as they began digging out the space for the pool. Within minutes they had a good portion of it dug, but then they stopped amid waved arms and yelling. I stepped outside to see what the commotion was.

Rick Jarvis, the contractor on the job, came up to me with a strange look on his face. "Mr. Sullivan, do you know anything about someone being buried on this property?"

I started to laugh, but it died in my throat as I realized he was serious. "No, of course not. Are you saying you found someone buried in my yard?"

He shrugged before taking off his hat and mopping his forehead with the back of his hand. "I dunno yet. The boys are still getting it up, but they think they hit a coffin down there."

The coffin was a seven-foot long, three foot wide wooden box that had been buried some ten feet down in our yard sometime before we had moved in a decade earlier. I felt the weight of dread and anxiety as they pulled the box free from the ground with yellow straps and slid it onto the grass a few feet away. One of the men approached Jarvis and told him they thought it was empty because it was so light, and after nodding, Jarvis turned back to me.

"It's your call, sir. It may be some weird old prank or something. We can open it up and see if anything is even inside, and if there's not, no harm no foul. We just go back to digging. Or we can go ahead and call the authorities, but that's going to slow things down whether there's a body in there or not."

I glanced at the partially-dug hole and the coffin. More time would mean more money. And it wouldn't hurt just to look. I turned back to the contractor and nodded. "Yeah, go ahead and check it out. No need to call somebody unless we find something."

Jarvis grinned and called a couple of his men over with a crowbar. With a bit of grunting and the squeal of rusty nails, they pried the top off the coffin. I stepped closer as the wooden lid fell aside and felt a surge of relief when I saw it was empty. Well, mostly empty. There were several sheets of paper scattered across the coffin floor as well as a small, mostly corroded metal flashlight that looked a good forty or fifty years old. Looking closer, one of the men also picked out a small black rock and the stub of an old wooden pencil.

Jarvis collected the items and held them out to me like an offering. "Where do you want me to put these things, sir? They're yours, after all." His expression was unreadable, but I could hear a wire of tension reverberating in his words. I almost told him to just throw it all away, but I had seen writing on those pages and was curious. So I just took the items and carried them inside. When I came back out, I stopped two men from dragging the coffin away, telling them that I'd take care of it. I didn't want them wasting any more time, and I hadn't decided what I wanted to do with it yet anyway. They had already set the lid back on top, so I dragged the entire thing around to the side of my garage before setting it down. As I did so, the lid slid off again and landed with the interior side face up for the first time.

The inside of the lid was covered in scratches. Darkly stained scratches that could have easily been old dried blood. My skin crawling, I leaned closer and saw what looked like a small piece of fingernail jutting out of one of the deep grooves in the stained wood. How was any of this possible? Surely it was all fake or there'd be a body, right?

Glancing around, I saw no one else could see the lid from where they were working, and I found myself secretly hoping they hadn't noticed it before. I wanted time to think before anyone started yelling that someone had been murdered or buried alive on the very spot I was planning on putting a pool for my little girls. Covering the coffin with a tarp from the garage, I went back inside to look at the items we had found.

The rock was a small, flat oval of smooth black stone, and holding it in the palm of my hand I was surprised by its weight and how cool it felt. It had an almost greasy texture to it, and after a few moments I put it down with mild disgust. The flashlight didn't work, of course, but from what I could make out of its shape underneath the green rust, it reminded me of flashlights I had seen at my grandfather's house as a child. He had worked as a plumber most of his life, and he always kept a large silver flashlight close at hand.

The pencil, such as it was, consisted of an inch-long nub of wood lacquered with faded green paint and stamped with barely legible letters in what was once gold foil. Part of the name had been obliterated by sharpening, but when I held it to the light coming through the window I could make out "Greenheart Ho". It didn't ring a bell, so I set it aside and began to glance through the papers. The paper was clearly old and of very high quality. It felt more like a bedsheet than paper I was used to, and I was impressed it had survived so long in the damp of the earth.

But not only had it survived, it was fairly legible. Most of the pages were filled with a neat, slanted pencil scrawl and clearly numbered as pages of a long letter. The last was written in larger, harsh slashes across the entirety of one sheet. The black lines of lead seemed to scream from the page:

DO NOT TAKE ANYTHING FROM THE COFFIN. BURY IT AGAIN AND FOREVER. DO NOT TOUCH THE STONE. DO NOT ANSWER THE GRAVEKEEPER.

My mouth went dry as I read the words. This didn't feel like some kind of strange joke, and my curiosity had curdled into an acid fear deep in my belly. At that moment, I felt certain in my actions, in my conviction that I needed to do what the message demanded, at least as best I could. I gathered up the other pages and pencil, intent on putting everything back in the coffin and telling them to rebury it. The pool could wait or go somewhere else. I'm not superstitious by nature, but something was very wrong with all of this and I wanted no part of it.

I stopped short when I realized I didn't see the stone. Swallowing hard, I checked under the table and all around the floor. As I grew more desperate and tried to allow for some miracle of physics that had led to the stone rolling a farther distance, I spread out my search as I tossed my living room and adjoining rooms for the small black rock. But nothing. It was just gone.

There was no chance someone had taken it. I had been standing less than two feet from it the entire time from when I set it down to when I saw it was missing. Still, I found myself considering asking the men outside anyway if anyone had seen it or taken it. I felt foolish at the thought, but my self-consciousness was being outpaced by my growing dread. Reaching for the door that led out to where they were working, I froze as I looked out the window.

All work had stopped and most of the men were gathering around Rick Jarvis, who was thrashing about on the ground as though he was having some kind of fit. My first thought was epilepsy, but then I realized he was screaming. He was clawing at his eyes as he wailed, and even from a distance I could see blood slinging off onto the freshly turned earth and surrounding work boots. And his men, his friends and workers, they weren't trying to help him at all. They were just watching.

Watching and laughing.

Part Two

I didn't go outside. I knew of no way I could help Jarvis, and I was terrified by what I was seeing. So instead I called 911 and waited by the window as the contractor's thrashing finally slowed and then stilled. The men around him had grown quiet now, standing motionless for several minutes until as one they began to glance at each other with some degree of confusion. There were four men out there aside from Jarvis, and I could have sworn from their expressions that they didn't understand what was going on or what they were doing. But they didn't move to help Jarvis either. Instead, they went slowly back to digging the hole as though their companion wasn't laying a few feet away, dead or dying.

They looked up dazedly at the approach of ambulance and deputy sirens, not showing any real apprehension or concern. Moving to the front door, I ran out and waved at the approaching vehicles, pointing around to the back of the house. The next few minutes were a flurry of activity. I was kept at the front of the house talking to a deputy, but I caught glimpses as two EMTs loaded Jarvis, still somehow alive, into the back of the ambulance while two other deputies questioned his men.

For my part, I told Deputy Ellison that I had seen Jarvis having a seizure and clawing at his face, and that his men had seemed to be acting strangely, but that I had not seen any of them actually try to hurt or help the man. All of this was true, but I left out any mention of the coffin or what we had found inside. I had thought about whether to go into these extra details with law enforcement or the EMTs while I waited for them to arrive, having given only bare bones details to the 911 operator when I called it in.

In my estimation, one of two things was true. Either there was something supernatural and sinister going on here or there wasn't. If there was, me telling other people about it would do little good except undermine my credibility and possibly have the other writings I hadn't looked at yet taken away from me. If everything had a mundane explanation, then the coffin and its contents were likely irrelevant. Even if the coffin had contained some kind of toxin, they would likely find it through testing Jarvis.

I knew there were holes in my reasoning, but I was still possessed by the feeling that the dire warning I had read was earnest and true, which meant I needed to assume I was dealing with something that I didn't understand and that wouldn't be understood by the average doctor or cop either. So I held things back, hoping it would all go away but knowing in the recesses of my heart that I wouldn't be so lucky.

Twenty minutes later I was driving to the hospital. Before I had left home, one of the other deputies had come up and told Ellison that the other men had given very little in the way of statements beyond that Jarvis had started having some kind of fit and they didn't know why. The deputy said with a meaningful look that based on their responses and demeanor, he had suggested they all get checked out medically, but they had refused treatment and started leaving the work site once he was done with his questions.

Ellison had clenched his jaw and nodded. "Just make sure you have all those birds' info so we can talk to them again." Turning to me, his expression softened slightly. "I can't make them see the doctor and don't have any reason to arrest them, but this is all very fishy sounding. I appreciate your help, and I'll be talking again to you soon."

I knew that Ellison didn't entirely trust what I had told him either, and I didn't blame him. As I turned into the hospital parking lot, I went back through what I had said for the tenth time, wanting to make sure I hadn't left out anything that might be helpful while not delving into those things I felt I needed to keep to myself.

Not able to think of anything, I stepped out of my car and headed into the visitor's entrance to the ER. I had hoped to see some of his workers coming to check on Jarvis as well, as that would at least give some indication of them having returned to normal, but no one came. For the next two hours I sat on an orange chair of molded plastic in the outdated and stale-smelling waiting room, my only company the drone of some afternoon talk show from a ceiling-mounted t.v. and a sad-looking old woman who sat on the opposite end of the room.

I wasn't even sure why I was there other than I felt somehow responsible for what had happened to Jarvis and I hoped that by staying I might either get some answers or at least absolve myself of some guilt. After the first hour, a doctor came out and told me that they had him stable and sedated, and they were planning on doing surgery that evening, but that since I wasn't family, it would probably be at least a day or two before I'd be able to go in and see him. When I asked if his eyes were going to be okay, the doctor had just given me a bleak look and said he couldn't discuss any medical details with me while shaking his head slowly side to side.

I felt sick to my stomach as he left. I debated leaving then, but I didn't really want to go back home and had no where else to be. So I sat, turning things over in my mind for several minutes before realizing with a start that I had the pages from the coffin with me. I had been worried about the deputies finding them, so I had gently folded and tucked them into my back pocket before they arrived. Pulling them out now, I glanced again at the page of screaming warnings before setting it aside. As far as I could tell, the rest of the sheets of paper were all one long letter, so I started reading it from the beginning as the day outside passed through soft twilight in its journey toward darkness.

To Whom It May Concern,

My name is Emily Thurman. I write this in the bedroom that has served as my prison for nearly twenty years, or at least as a cell within the larger prison that is this house, this family, this existence. I was treated well-enough for the first two decades of my life, for during that period I played the role of a dutiful daughter in a well-to-do family as was expected. When my uncle Frederick attempted to interfere with me sexually was the night that my troubles began.

He was not held to account thanks to my father's misogyny and my mother's desire for her brother's favor and business acumen. Even then our family was heading for shallower waters financially, and this was more than two decades before the collapse of 1929. For my part, I was treated coldly for my accusations if not called an outright liar. This caused me more than a little distress, but I had resolved to marshal my resources and leave the cooling embrace of my family for leaner, but hopefully greener, pastures elsewhere as soon as possible.

Then one night in January of 1909, three months after the incident with my uncle, I found myself woken roughly by strange men. My first thoughts were of robbery or abduction, but as I was carried through the house, I saw my family standing by and watching. Father looked troubled but stood silent. Mother and Frederick stared blankly into the distance as I was carried by them, screaming and thrashing against my captors. It was all for naught. I was thrust into a waiting motor car that marked the beginning of my journey to Greenheart Home.

Greenheart Home, as I would soon learn, was a private institution tucked away like a handmaiden's secret in the black woods of northern California. One could call it a mental ward, a retreat, or a prison and not be wrong. But Greenheart's true purpose was as a place of forgetting. Wealthy and prominent families would send their troubled children, their embarrassing parents, their undesirable mistakes to Greenheart, and there they would stay under the guise of mercy and the pretense of establishment.

My official diagnosis at Greenheart Home was "melancholia and female disease", as though being a woman was some kind of blight in and of itself. Those first few weeks I railed against every encounter, demanding my freedom or at least to speak to someone in control. Over time I learned that my freedom had died as soon as I spoke out against my uncle, and that whoever was in control, the salient point was that it was not me.

This led, as one might imagine, to a period of depression. Greenheart was not an unpleasant place aesthetically, as keeping up appearances *and salving the conscience of those families that dumped their refuse here required a certain veneer of comfort and respectability. But a gilded cage is still a cage, and I wanted no part of any of it. My attempts to escape were foiled, and eventually my period of despair became burdensome in its own right, so one day I woke up resolved to make a kind of life in that place.*

I had shunned most social contact since my arrival, but once I opened myself up to the other women there, I found several fast friends. Just to be able to talk to people again, particularly others that shared my plight, was a blessing. In some ways, the next two years were the best of my life, as bizarre as that might seem from the outside. Living at Greenheart was much like living most places, in that eventually you grow accustomed to things you would have never thought possible.

At any given time there were around 150 women and young girls at Greenheart Home, and the fact that periodically people would be gone without warning, never to return, seemed strange but not sinister. We would be told their family had sent for them and that would be the end of it. We had no way to dispute it, and no recourse even if we had the desire. It wasn't until later that we began to realize what was really happening to our fellow inmates.

The ruler of that terrible little kingdom was a man named Dr. Chester Middleton, a psychologist of some esteem to hear the nurses tell it, though the only times we ever saw him was passing through as he spoke to this nurse or that orderly, occasionally at mandated functions, and the night of the fire that ended it all in 1911. But even before that night, there was always a tension in the air at Greenheart. A hidden power struggle between two unlikely opponents: The head doctor and the gardener.

Elias Meeks was a large and sullen man with a stormy disposition and a thick Eastern European accent that seemed to come and go depending on whether he wanted you to understand his dark mutterings or not. He had apparently been the groundskeeper at Greenheart Home for a number of years, and to a person, everyone seemed to be terrified of him. Mostly this was a subtle thing— the staff would avoid him whenever possible, avoiding his eyes when he approached. For Meeks' part, he radiated a feeling of menace like living heat, but I never saw him be actively cruel or violent with anyone, which was more than I could say for some of the nurses and orderlies.

But that did little to lessen our fear of him. We would watch him cutting the grass or repairing the roof, and my small group of friends would instinctively pull closer together as we hustled past. He would occasionally take special care with the private cemetery at the edge of the grounds, and it was from this that he earned the nickname that we all called him by when he was out of earshot. The Gravekeeper.

I let out a small gasp as I felt my cellphone vibrating in my pocket. Pulling it out, I didn't recognize the number but decided I should answer given the day I was having. It was Deputy Ellison.

"Where are you at, Mr. Sullivan?"

"I'm still at the hospital. The ER waiting room. Why?"

There was a pause and I could tell the deputy was debating how much he should say. Letting out a deep breath, he went on. "Because out of those four guys out there with you and Jarvis today, two of them went home and murdered their families in the last hour. We've got BOLOs out on the other two, and I was about to put one out on you if I couldn't get ahold of you."

I couldn't breathe. How was any of this possible? I...

"You still there, Mr. Sullivan?"

"Yes...yes, I'm here. They...they killed their families?"

I could hear the weariness in the other man's voice. "Yeah. Worse thing I've ever seen. We had to shoot one of them down and the other is still holed up in his house, but as far as we can tell, we have at least six dead so far. Seven if Jarvis doesn't make it."

I was about to tell him what the doctor had told me when the lights went out, plunging the waiting room into total darkness. After a moment a couple of security lights flickered on fitfully, but no more. Looking around, I saw no people or any of the normal noises I would expect in a hospital. Even the little old woman had left at some point. It was like I was in a tomb.

"Deputy...the power just went out here in the hospital. It's dark."

Another moment of contemplative silence and then his voice was back, shot through with anger and fear. "That's impossible. Even if the hospital loses power, the back-up gennies would kick in within less than a second. There's too much that can go wrong if they really lose power."

I gritted my teeth as I started slowly making my way to the double-doors that led into the deeper bowels of the hospital. Peering through the narrow windows in the doors, I saw only darkness punctuated by two dim and flickering security lights on my end of the hallway. The other end was utterly black and devoid of life.

"I'm fucking telling you it's dark. No lights outside either as far as I can tell. And I don't see any people. It's like a ghost town in here. I'm leaving, but you should get someone over here."

"No," the deputy said, his voice more shrill this time. "You stay put. You're either a potential victim or a potential suspect, but either way you and me are going to talk more before you go anywhere. On my way." With that he hung up and I found myself staring dumbfounded at my phone. It took me only a moment of internal debate to decide he could go fuck himself and that I'd see him later when I wasn't scared out of my mind. Something was terribly wrong here and I was leaving.

That's when I heard the voice from somewhere deep in the shadows. In the moment it took for me to register it fully, I felt a surge of relief at having contact with another person. Then I realized who was speaking to me from some nearby darkened hall. It was Rick Jarvis. His voice was strange and gravelly, and he had a strange lilt to his words that I didn't remember from my prior conversations with him, but it was him all right. And he was calling to me.

"I know yer out there, Sully. I may not can see ya, but that's all right. Yes, that's all right."

He trailed off in a wet, uneven croon, almost as though he was lost in thought. Then he was back, his voice brighter and closer sounding. "Yeah, I can't see ya, but I can smell ya, Sully. Just stay where you are and I'll be with ya shortly."

My heart thudding in my chest, I turned to run towards the exit just as I heard a metallic clunk ring through the doors. I hit them hard and bounced off, the magnetic locks giving very little as I shoved against them again and again. After my fifth attempt I stopped, forcing myself to slow down and think. Slow down and listen. There had to be emergency exits they couldn't lock like this. That HE couldn't lock like this. I just had to avoid him for...

"There ya are, my boy." The voice was right behind me now, loud as a gunshot in the dark. **"Now. Let's get to know each other better."**

Part Three

I had never really been afraid before. I thought I had. When I was bit by a snake when I was seven. The night I got sideswiped by a semi coming home from college and had to wait until the fire department could cut me out of my ruined car. The first time I realized Sandra didn't love me any more.

Those were all frightening, but they were mainly a mixture of pain and surprise—my body's adrenaline and my mind's expectations being thrown into chaos. A moment of peril that time and distance would turn into forgotten trauma or an interesting story. A scar or a monument not to the danger, but to my surviving it.

When the thing that had once been Rick Jarvis slammed me against the doors of the emergency room at Richland County Hospital, my vision blurred as tears of pain and terror flooded my eyes. The parking lot beyond was dark, but in the distance I could see the lights of a gas station at the nearest intersection. It could have been on the moon and not felt farther away. A hand pressed my forehead against the glass painfully even as his body pinned me against the release bar of the door.

I heard myself let out some kind of short animal squeal as I tried to wriggle free, but I didn't struggle for long. For one thing, I could tell he was far stronger than me. For another, I could feel the first touches of true fear as its cold fingers caressed my heart.

True fear isn't about being hurt. It isn't about losing your belongings or even your life. True fear is about losing yourself. What you are, what you were, what you love. It's the feeling of a beast hungrily roaming the rooms of your heart, a nameless despair that has finished eating your hope and has moved on to your soul.

As I felt the thing I'd come to know as the Gravekeeper breathing hot, fetid breath into my ear, I understood being afraid. As he chuckled, digging his fingers into my ribs, lightly at first and then hard enough that I felt wet, hot pain on my right side, I could sympathize with my brain's flight into sheer animal terror. When I realized how excited and happy he was, how aroused and joyous my pain and fear made him as he pressed himself tight and began digging into me, I felt myself sliding towards a slavering abyss.

You need to understand that I was crying and slobbering during all of this, begging to be let go. We were in a vacuum of fear and pain— dignity and pride had no chance of survival in such harsh conditions. In the moment I felt like I would have done anything just to get his burning hands off of me, his probing fingers out of my side. But there was something more than that, worse than that, occurring at the same time. In the still darkness of my inner self, there was a moment of contact and recoil. Like a field mouse scenting a snake in its burrow, my spirit, delicate and shuddering, somehow recognized the rotten thing that hid in that poor man's meat. And in that moment, I think my soul glimpsed its eventual doom.

"So are ya scared enough now, Sully? Starting to understand? Are ya ready to quit running and get down to bibs and bobs, my boy?" A new wash of rotting breath hit me and I found myself wondering absently if the man pinning me to the door was already dead. I almost answered automatically. As I said, I'd already been begging, but this was the first time he had asked me a direct question in the eternity since he had first found me in the dark.

DO NOT ANSWER THE GRAVEKEEPER

The words blazed across my mind and I kept silent. Several seconds passed and then I was suddenly free. I let out a gasp as though coming up for air before turning around. I had no idea of fighting back or even trying to defend myself. But I did want to see him for some reason, as though it would bring some kind of understanding. I was disappointed at first, his face and form lost in shadow beyond a dim outline. The security lights in the room were behind him and so weak that the light did little but make him a more tangible bit of darkness.

Then his face was lit by alternating blossoms of white and blue light. I sucked in an involuntary breath at the sight of him. His skin seemed impossibly dry and hard, as though it was made from some kind of malleable resin or polished stone. His eyes...where his eyes should be...were raw red pits of ruined flesh riddled with…I wasn't sure. It reminded me of a picture I had seen once of a cave lined with jagged quartz—sharp crystals growing towards each other, digging through the meat of the earth to form something new in the void. But where the picture had been strangely beautiful, this was the opposite. It was some kind of unnatural decay.

"Step back from the fucking door, Sullivan!"

Turning, I realized that Deputy Ellison had been trying to get through the door for several seconds. I took several steps back and he slammed a collapsible baton into the glass sharply. Glancing at the Jarvis-thing, I saw he was just standing there passively, as though he was waiting for something. A second strike and the glass was spiderwebbed. A third and it went cloudy before tumbling free of the frame.

"Both of you get down on the ground! Now!"

I went to obey but hesitated. I didn't want to get on the ground with that monster so close by. To my surprise, he was already getting down on his hands and knees, a small smile crawling onto his rigid lips, causing them to crack and bleed as it widened. He whispered across the distance to me in a tone that seemed on the edge of laughter.

"Don't you worry, Sully. We'll be together again real soon."

"Three more people, Mr. Sullivan. Two nurses and a doctor. Dead. Killed by that maniac Jarvis, despite him having...whatever he has wrong with him. On top of that, another twenty staff and patients that were unconscious for nearly two hours with no memory of what happened. So today, in a town that considers it something if we have two murders a year, we've got ten people dead in one day. Because, before I forget, we had to kill the second worker who spontaneously decided his entire family needed to die today." I could see Ellison was struggling to maintain his composure, trying to do his job of interrogating me while being far out of his depth and understanding. I sympathized, but I didn't have any answers either. At least not yet.

I sighed. "Look, I don't know what's going on any more than you..."

"Bullshit!" he yelled, throwing down a plastic evidence bag that contained what I recognized as the pages of the letter. In my panic at the hospital I had forgotten them in the waiting room, and by the time I had remembered, it was too late. "I don't know what this shit is, but I can tell from glancing at it that it's old and strange. Just like that coffin you had those men digging up today." My eyes widened and he smiled bitterly. "Oh yeah, we know about that now too. I sent a unit back to your house and they found where you had hidden it. Could see the fresh dirt on it and put two and two together. We're a small department, but we're not idiots. And you need to stop treating us like we are."

I sat back in my chair and sighed. "Listen, I don't think you're stupid. I just don't know what's going on and I'm trying to figure it out. But you need to hear what I'm saying. That thing you arrested...it's not Jarvis. It's some kind of monster. You need to kill it or bury it somewhere deep if it won't die."

The deputy sat down across the table from me. The interview room was well-lit, and I could see the exhaustion and fear on his face, but his voice was steady when he spoke. "You don't have to convince me that something abnormal is going on, or that the fucker is a monster. But we don't execute people, even if they deserve it. He's locked up tight, and aside from getting him checked out medically in the morning, his ass won't leave that cell until he's before a judge on Monday. You have my word."

I shook my head. "That won't work. He's strong and he can affect people. Make them do things. I don't know what he is, but we aren't safe here."

Ellison was going to respond further when he got a call on his cell phone. "I'm in the middle of...What? That's not...Who was down there with him?" The color was draining from his face as he spoke, and he was already heading toward the door as he talked. Almost as an afterthought he turned to me and pointed. "Keep your ass in here. I'll be right back."

I felt my stomach knotting as I waited. I considered leaving, but I didn't know that running would help anything. Shifting in my chair, I felt a flare of fresh pain in my side and grunted. They had cleaned the wound and put a bandage on it, but they asked me to hold off taking any pain meds until my interview was done. I'd agreed at the time, but now I was starting to regret it.

I jumped when the door suddenly swung open. I was expecting either Ellison or the monster, but it was a younger female deputy instead. She smiled as she came in and gave me a can of ginger ale. "Sorry this is taking so long. Very chaotic at the moment."

I smiled weakly at her. "What's going on? Deputy Ellison just went running out of here a few minutes ago like there was an emergency."

The girl looked down and then glanced at the camera mounted in the corner of the room. "I really shouldn't say anything."

"Please. I'm really freaking out in here. Anything you can tell me."

She nodded and sat down across from me. "Well, the guy they brought in with you, the murder suspect? They were keeping him in a holding cell downstairs. Locked tight, camera in the cell, the whole nine yards. And now he's gone. Escaped somehow, but no one knows how. The only thing they found was some kind of weird rock sitting on the bench in the cell."

I stood up suddenly, knocking my chair over as I backed to the wall. "Fuck. Fuck! I told him! I...we have to get out of here, we're not safe, we have to..."

The deputy was wide-eyed as she stood and retreated to the door. "Look, I shouldn't have said anything. Just calm down. We're safer here than anywhere. Trust me, if that guy was still in the station, we would know it. Just stay here and I'll get Ellison for you." She paused and then added, "Just please don't tell them what I told you. I need my job."

I took a deep breath and tried to get control of myself. "Yeah. Yeah, your secret is safe with me. I'm sorry. I just...I hope you find him soon. He's very dangerous."

She nodded, her face solemn. "I believe you. We'll probably be calling in the state police on this one anyway." She opened the door but stopped halfway through, turning back to me. "Hey, you want any ice with that drink?"

I waved my hand. "No, no this is fine. Thank you."

The girl's face hardened as her lips peeled away from her teeth in a mockery of a smile. The voice that came from her was rough and unnatural, but I recognized it right away.

"That's two, Sully." A thin line of drool began to drip out of the corner of the girl's mouth as it spoke. "I'm crawling towards you, my boy. Going to crawl right up inside you to stay, I think." The thing wiped the drool away absently as it looked at me with her unblinking hazel eyes. **"Yes...I think right up inside you to stay."**

Part Four

I'd expected that she was going to close the door back and attack me, but instead it just waved and walked out of sight down the hallway. I considered running out screaming, but I worried that might provoke the thing inside the young deputy, so instead I kept my back against the far wall of the interrogation room and called Deputy Ellison on my phone.

I told him what had happened in a brief whisper and he said he was on his way. True to his word, less than a minute later he was running into the room. Shutting the door, he looked at me with anxious frustration. "Have you seen her again?"

I paused, weighing if this could be another trick, the Gravekeeper having taken over Ellison now, but decided it seemed unlikely and worth the risk to trust Ellison for the moment. I shook my head. "No, she just told me about Jarvis disappearing, tricked me into answering a question, and seemed satisfied with that. She left out of here going to the right and I was scared to follow her."

He nodded. "I don't blame you. Based on your description, I had the front desk check for any female deputies that left in the last few minutes. Rachel Minas left in a hurry just a minute ago. I told dispatch to get ahold of her, but I don't know how likely that is based on what you're telling me." He sat down at the table with a sigh and gestured to the other chair. "Look, I know something fucked up is going on, and I'm past thinking it's likely that it's your fault. But you're clearly involved whether you want to be or not. It wants something from you. So if you have any more information, now's the time to give it to me."

Sitting down across from him, I recounted the details I had omitted earlier about what had happened at the house, as well as what I had read so far in the letter from the coffin. Ellison listened intently, not speaking after I had been finished for close to a minute.

"Okay, well, several things. First, you should have told me all this to start with. It might not have helped anything, but it wouldn't have hurt. Second, the way the items were in the coffin makes sense...or well, it doesn't make sense, but it's consistent with a theory I had about Jarvis."

I frowned at him. "What was your theory?"

He puffed out a long breath. "That he didn't escape. That he just...went away. I don't really know what that means yet, but I saw no way how he could have gotten out of that room short of teleportation, and I saw no reason why he would leave a souvenir behind either. Because Minas wasn't lying about the rock. We found one in the cell, just like you described from the coffin. And then, with me watching it as another deputy went to go get an evidence bag, it just vanished into thin air." Scrubbing his hand through his hair, he went on. "The thing is, Minas was never in that cell with him. Or with the rock. As far as I know, she wasn't even in the jail section of the sheriff's office. She's a road deputy and had just come back from the end of a shift."

I didn't know what to make of that. I'd always assumed that the rock was somehow tied to people getting taken over by the thing, but that seemed unlikely if what he was saying was true.

A thought occurred to me. "Was she at one of the workers' houses when you were dealing with them? Maybe she got 'infected' there somehow?"

Ellison shook his head. "No, she's a good deputy, but green. Hasn't been on the road six months. She was one of the few we kept out on normal patrol while we were dealing with all this other." He tapped the bag containing the letter. "You say there's more you haven't read?"

"Yes, I got interrupted by Jarvis at the hospital." I shuddered involuntarily at the memory and tried to push it away. "We should finish it and see if it gives us any ideas."

Glancing at his cell phone, he pushed the bag to me. "Go ahead. Just read it out loud."

The first time that we witnessed the strange power dynamic between the Gravekeeper and Dr. Middleton was during one of our rare social interactions with the Men's Ward at Greenheart Home. For various reason, there was generally strict segregation between the sexes, with separate wings, dining halls, and recreational areas for women and men. For the most part, it was easy to forget that they were even there, and that was typically preferable.

The monthly picnic on the vast front lawn of Greenheart was always an ordeal. Some of the women eagerly anticipated the day, putting extra effort into their appearance and making every attempt to garner attention from one or more men during the three hours we were together. For me, it amounted to huddling amongst my friends and trying to avoid eye contact with those men that were actively looking for female companionship. While the picnic was supervised, our caretakers were far from assiduous, and I came to understand that they would deliberately turn a blind eye if a couple wandered off into one of the distant stands of trees or bushes closer to the outer perimeter fence. There was no way for them to escape, after all, and if some indiscretion led to a pregnancy, they had means of profiting from that as well.

It should be clear that I do not hate men—far from it. But I've never seen much benefit in purely physical congress of that sort, and it wasn't as though I could establish a relationship with someone that I saw briefly once a month. While I pitied their plight as I did my own, I had no desire to be an outlet for some stranger's pent up lust.

So I resigned myself to small conversations with my friends, watching the clouds, and reading the latest book I would get out of the lending library. I enjoyed poetry the best, and on this particular day I was reading, funnily enough, MEN AND WOMEN by Robert Browning. I was thoroughly engrossed, but I looked up when I heard a commotion up near the top of the lawn near the building.

"Ya think yer clever, doctor?" The Gravekeeper's accent was light but his voice laden with threat as it rolled across the grass. He was talking to Dr. Middleton, who took a step back as he raised his hands.

"I don't know what you mean, Meeks." I could hear anger in the man's voice, but it broke as he said the Gravekeeper's name.

Meeks let out a wet, nasty laugh. "Oh, ya know well enough I think. Yes, I think ya do." He took a step toward the doctor, who retreated in kind. "Ya think I don't know about yer lil' side ventures?" He looked off in the distance for several moments, to the point I thought Dr. Middleton was going to respond before he was cut off by the Gravekeeper's next words. "I do. I do. I don't care about the babbies, but I do about the trucks, you ken? Ya stop 'em, or I'll stop YOU." As he said the last, I had the odd image of a hand stopping the pendulum of a clock, killing its motion, its life. I learned later that several of my friends who watched the scene unfold had the exact same image as I.

One of the head nurses headed over to the argument, presumably to help the crumbling Dr. Middleton, but the Gravekeeper turned his gaze on her, pinning her to the spot. "This lil' soiree is over, nurse. I want everyone back inside, now. Need peace and quiet on my lawn so I can hear myself think."

The older woman's mouth moved wordlessly as she turned to glance at the doctor. Even at a distance you could tell by his rounded shoulders and the way he ignored looking at her that he was beaten. "Yes. Um, yes, let's cut it short this month. I have too much work to do." Dejected, the nurse turned and started calling for the nurses to collect their charges and return them to their respective chambers in the Greenheart.

We gathered up our things and headed for the building, but as we approached the top of the lawn, I felt something at my core tremble. I turned and saw the Gravekeeper looking at me, his dark eyes steady as the deathwatch gaze of a crocodile or an angler fish—seeing and not seeing at the same time. My heart leapt, and then leapt again when his gaze followed my movements.

"What're ya looking at, my girl?" He pronounced the last "GULL". His voice was rough and deep, and at such proximity, it took all I had not to run at hearing it.

Turning away from him, I lowered my head and murmured, "Nothing." Most of my attention was on keeping my steps measured as I crossed the threshold into the building, on not showing the *fear I felt. But then I heard his chuckle behind me as he muttered something low.*

What I feared then was confirmed over time—I had been somehow marked by the thing we called the Gravekeeper. As for his low muttering, it didn't make sense to me when I was at Greenheart, but sitting here in the spring of 1931, I see its significance all too clearly.

"That's one, my pet. Yes, I think that's one."

I looked up at Ellison. "This is the same kind of shit he was saying to me. Or she was...Minas...but you know what I mean. It's something to do with tricking some people into answering him several times. I don't know why it's not like that for everybody, but it can't be. From what you're saying, that deputy would have never even seen him."

He nodded, his face drawn. "Yeah. I mean, no, she wouldn't have ever had a chance to be asked shit by Jarvis. Fuck...keep going. I want to know how we stop this fucker, and this is all we have to go on."

I knew from the pages I was holding there wasn't much left, and my heart sank at the realization. I had been hoping that this letter from the past would hold some hidden key to how to stop this thing. That's what always happened in horror movies, right? You just had to put the puzzle together and your reward would be the thing that could slay the beast.

But there was no point in dampening our spirits more by saying it out loud. Instead, I finished the letter.

Over the next several months, I saw and heard gossip of several more confrontations between Meeks and Dr. Middleton. In most of them, it seemed the Gravekeeper's primary point was to shame and cow the doctor, but there did seem to be some common thread regarding something the doctor was doing that Meeks didn't like. It wasn't until Christmas Eve of 1911 that I fully understood what that was.

We were all gathered in the dining hall having our dinner—roasted geese, figgy pudding, and bowls of steaming potatoes filled every table, and despite our situation, the mood in the room was actually something close to merry. Dr. Middleton sat at the head table, sourly picking at his food while pretending to pay attention to one of the other doctors that had come on at Greenheart just a few months prior. The head doctor's face changed as the doors at the opposite end of the room banged open.

It was the Gravekeeper. He strode down the middle of the long hall, and I shuddered as he spared me a knowing glance in his passing.

Without any real effort, he leapt the five feet onto the raised platform where the head table sat, his hands loose at his sides like a gunfighter from the stories my father would read me as a little girl.

"I told ya, Doc. But ya thought ya knew better. Thought ya were smart and could fool me."

Middleton visibly paled. "I...I don't know what you mean, Meeks."

I heard that rough chuckle again. "Sure ya do. Ya kept sending out our cattle here." He gestured back in our direction. "Sending 'em to another butcher." He suddenly slammed a fist down on the table, caving it in and sending food flying amid screams of terror and shuffling feet. The Gravekeeper's voice somehow carried over the commotion, and I wonder now if he was speaking at all, or if I was hearing him in my mind.

"But I'm a greedy, selfish butcher. Greedy and so very hungry."

Middleton's face went red with anger. "Shut up, you fool! You'll ruin us both!"

I watched as Meeks' hand shot forward and through the doctor's head. Bone and viscera exploded out onto the other staff that were now scrambling desperately off their platform and toward the doors.

"I don't want to share, ya see? Never have. So I think it's time to start fresh." He turned around to face us, slinging his arm hard enough that meat and gore splashed against the far wall. "Yes, I think it's time for a change." A number of staff and inmates were at the doors by now, but they couldn't escape. Only the door nearest me seemed to be open, and people flooded out of it as flames began to appear along the walls and tables.

I had been somewhat transfixed by the horror unfolding before us, but the warmth of the fire brought me to my senses. I pushed away from the table and headed for the door, pushing my way through the crowd and out into the cold night air. Even through the crackling of the flame-wreathed walls and the distance we had moved from the building, I thought I could hear Meeks laughing.

Nearly forty people died that night. By the next morning I was on a train headed back here to my family. My trip was uneventful, and my return home was unceremonious. There was no discussion of Greenheart Home or my unwilling confinement there. Life had moved on without me, and carrying the perspective I had gained at Greenheart Home, I found myself grateful for being removed from it. I missed my friends terribly, but never saw or heard from them again. I was told in blunt terms by my mother that I was welcome to stay as long as I behaved, but if there were any further problems, or if I attempted to leave my family's tender care, they would see me put in a state hospital that would make Greenheart seem like a paradise. The certain reality of that threat terrified me, and to my shame, kept me a largely silent and docile prisoner over these years.

I quickly divorced myself from all but mandatory family functions, staying mainly in my room or the library at times when I knew others weren't apt to be around. I was like a ghost haunting my own home, and that separation was a comfort. I lost myself in books and writing poetry, and occasionally talking to a distant aunt on our new telephone. She had no ability to help my predicament, but she was a kind voice in the dark nonetheless, and while I was initially put off by the alien means of communication, I soon came to look forward to her calls once every week or two.

The last of my calls with my aunt was strange from the beginning. She seemed uninterested in what I was saying and her manner of speech seemed somewhat abnormal. I was wondering if she was sick or preoccupied by some trouble when I realized she was asking me a question.

"Would you like me to come and visit you, Emily?"

My chest flared with happiness. I had wanted to ask her for months, but was afraid that the suggestion might have the opposite effect of pushing her away. Trying to not sound overeager, I paused before breathlessly answering yes.

There was a strange smacking sound on the other end of the line. "Ah, there we are. That's two, my girl. Don't ya worry. I'll be visiting ya real soon to get the last one."

I had dropped the phone with a clatter and ran from the house, but to no avail. I was caught, I was locked in, and I was just watched closer afterward, my family apparently having warmed to the idea of acting as my wardens and preferring it to the embarrassment of public institutions. It was in this trap that I stayed, waiting for him to come—waiting for IT to come— for how could such a thing be human? I heard some days after my last phone call that my aunt had taken her own life, but I knew the lie of it. That thing had murdered her and was coming for me next.

Except it never came. Years passed, and as time dulled the edge of my fear and trepidations, the banality of my existence made me almost pine for something as strange as whatever the

Gravekeeper might be. Of course, that was a foolish wish, but it was one that was soon granted.

It was my mother this time, asking if I wanted any lunch, and as soon as I answered I felt the change come over me. It felt as though someone had set fire to my brain. I stumbled back from the threshold of my room and collapsed against my bed, sliding to the floor as the world receded to black.

When I awoke, I knew I was ruined. Tainted. I could feel him nesting in my mind, in my soul. He didn't take control often, but I could feel him sending out tendrils as he probed my thoughts and feelings. I began to have dark and perverse thoughts, as well as the reoccurring image of a face that was both Meeks and not Meeks, its mouth a red slash full of broken knives cutting and re-cutting the long, purplish tongue that lolled out of its mouth, wet and hungry.

I could feel that mouth in my mind, consuming me bit by bit, replacing me with something else. I could feel that dark tongue roving and questing, burning everything with its acid touch. I could feel it licking the inner chambers of my heart.

My mother is dead now, and they've decided I'm to blame. The past two weeks have convinced them that I'm evil—possibly possessed. As I don't remember spans of that time, and given what I know, who am I to argue?

They mean to bury me. Bury me and leave this house forever, though whether that last idea is truly theirs or the bank's, that's another matter. I wish I had it in me to fight them, but I'm too tired. And considering what lives inside me now, perhaps it's the best thing.

I always wrote such happy poems. I was embarrassed to have anyone read them because of their optimism and bright view of a world beyond the borders of places like Greenheart Home or my own family. Perhaps the idea that there are good people and good places—places where truth and love and kindness can find light enough to grow tall and strong—is a fantasy, but I don't think so. I just think it's foreclosed to me now.

Last night I woke to find that a new poem had been written. HIS poem, not mine.

The Magpie Song

There's a flock of magpies round me, round me,
They soar as high as you see, you see,
They took my eyes, but fairly paid,
For I rest in their eyes as even trade,
Spanning the land and the sea, the sea,

There's a flock of blackbirds in flight, in flight,
They move to and fro every night, every night,
They took my ears, beaks sharp and wry,
But it favors me with each sobbing cry,
Found in the spaces away from the light, the light,

There's a flock of crows crying loud, crying loud,
They cast shadows great as a cloud, a shroud,
They took my tongue, and so my voice,
By then I was strong--they had no choice,
It's with their pink darts I taste the tears, the tears.

There's a sky full of rooks and it's me, it's me,
See the remains in the field I used to be, used to be,
But now I move free, still young and hungry,
Still reaching out into the void.

I see you.

Shining there.

Your spirit.

Unaware.

I think he wrote it at least in part to mock me. To twist something that I love and show me how he's going to taint every corner of my life, letting me watch until it's all gone. But I've lived a small life. I blame my family for some of that, but

I can't lay it all at their door. Perhaps I should have been braver and bolder. Stronger. I should have found a way.

But it's too late for me now. They mean to bury me tonight. As horrible as that is, I won't fight them. The one benefit of having such a small life is that it is easier to risk it, easier to finally be brave. I'll gladly give my life if I can carry the Gravekeeper with me. Keep him…it from touching others. Protect the goodness that I know is out there somewhere in the world.

I hear them coming for me now so I must end this. I will try to hide this on my person as well as the means to write more if I have the need and the ability. I've just realized what I've been writing this all with. I don't remember this pencil, and I wonder where

---

"It ends there." My mouth was dry and I felt on the verge of tears, both for Emily and for myself. I felt no closer to a solution, and I could tell Ellison felt the same. We stared at each other for a moment before I asked a question that had been in the back of my mind since I started reading us the rest of the letter, "Why do you believe me? Why do you believe any of this?" I laid the letter down and sat back. "I could just be crazy or a liar. I could have faked this letter, be giving these people bath salts or something. So why are you so willing to believe that the Gravekeeper is real?"

Ellison rubbed his mouth and gave me a wan smile. "I'd like to say it's just my gut. My cop's instinct. But my instincts have never been that great, if I'm honest. The real reason is because this isn't the first time I've ever seen a monster." I raised an eyebrow and he went on. "Not this thing. Nothing like this thing, whatever it is. But there was a time when my brother got taken by someone. Some thing. I was a teenager at the time, and I was stupid. Thought I'd track him down, hunt down whoever took him. Wound up, I was the one being hunted."

"I got drug to the place where it had my brother—turns out I hadn't been too far off, but I was too late. He was torn apart." I saw tears welling in his eyes as he looked away to the wall. "Suddenly this man was there. He killed that thing and saved me."

I leaned forward, my eyes wide. "How did he kill it? Maybe that'll help us."

He laughed softly. "You'll think I'm lying, but he killed it with a crowbar and an electric drill. When he was done, it was just gone. Disappeared. Before today, it was the most bizarre thing I'd ever seen, and it's still a close second."

I went to ask something else but my phone rang. It was Sandra. And she was screaming.

Part Five

I drove behind Deputy Ellison, his patrol car's lights forging us a path as we sped through town and out to the interstate. All we had to go on were three words Sandra had said in the middle of her terrified screaming. "At Hideaway Lodge." I didn't understand the reference, but Ellison told me Hideaway Lodge was a large motel along the interstate. When I learned it lay somewhere between my town and where Sandra was living with the girls, it made more sense. It also drove home that it might not just be her in jeopardy, but our daughters Alice and Kristi as well.

Half out of my mind with fear, I was running out of the building when Ellison caught me. "You need to take a breath, man." I tried to pull away, but he held me fast. "I know, and we're going to go get them. But you aren't good to anybody if you kill yourself getting there. Let me help."

I shook my head. "No, no cops. I'm going to do what I have to do, and I can't have someone between me and them. I can't let this keep going on."

Ellison smiled, his eyes hard but not unfriendly. "I'm not talking about cops. I know enough to know this is something special. Like when that thing got my brother. I'm not helping you as a deputy." He glanced out the window to the parking lot. "Though I'm not above running the sirens to get us there faster."

We pulled into the gravel parking lot in a cloud of grey dust, and Ellison was already in the office before I was fully out of my car. I almost followed him in, but held back out of fear that a harried civilian partner would only weaken his authority. In a minute he was back out and heading toward me.

"Guy said that two men checked in about two hours ago. He said there may have been other people in the car, but he never got a good look. Then, half an hour ago he saw a patrol car pull up." He pointed down to the corner of the building. "That's Minas' patrol unit. The motel manager never saw her, but he said the car hasn't moved that he's noticed since it arrived." Ellison glanced worriedly up at the fourth floor of the motel. "Based on how he described the men, I think we just found the last two of Jarvis' workers."

"What's the room number?" I could hear the barely restrained anger in my voice. I had been trying to be patient, but I needed to get up there now and he was wasting time.

He glanced back at me. "I'm getting to that, but first you need to hear me. We're likely walking into a hostage situation with two homicidal maniacs and a trained, armed officer with a monster in her brain. Best case scenario, I'm probably going to be fired. Worst case, most of us wind up dead or puppets for that damned thing. I'm not trying to be a hero here, but you need to follow my lead. Listen to what I tell you to do and stay out of my line of sight on them at all times. You clear?" I nodded and he patted me on the shoulder. "Okay, let's go get your family back. They're in Room 403."

We went up the stairs slowly, looking around constantly for a nearby ambush or a distant threat. But there was nothing. If there was anyone else even staying at the massive motel, you couldn't tell it by what we saw as we ascended to the fourth floor. We reached 403 and I went to knock, but Ellison shook his head. He gently pushed me to one side of the door as he moved to the other. Once in position, he drew his gun and quietly tried the knob.

The door opened easily into a well-lit room. On the bed was Sandra and the girls, their hands tied in front of them and pieces of ripped bedsheet tied across their mouths as gags.

Standing on either side of them like bodyguards were the last two men from when the coffin was found. They were both caked with dirt and filthy, and I could tell from their clothes that they had recently urinated on themselves. As we stepped into the room, the smell of rotten meat and shit emanating from them made me gag. For their part, they barely even glanced at us as we entered, their eyes only ticking in our direction briefly as they continued their slack-faced manning of the post.

Ellison gestured for me to stay back as he checked the small bathroom just inside the entry door. A moment later he was back out and into the room proper. Looking around, he saw what I saw. No Deputy Minas. Holding his gun on the men, he edged around them to glance out at the small balcony that looked out onto a dismal clump of scrub pines. She wasn't hiding out there either.

Then I saw it.

"The rock's back." I pointed to the room's television stand. A couple of inches in front of the t.v. was the smooth flat stone. I had the crazy urge to pick it up, open the sliding glass door and hurl it out into the woods. But I knew it would do no good. There was no stopping this. Just containing it. I had to get it away from the others.

"Put your hands on your head and step to the front door. When you reach the outside of the door, get down on the ground. If you do anything else, I WILL fucking shoot you."

I looked up and saw that Ellison was trying to get the workers out of the room. Sandra and the girls had been squealing with some mixture of joy and fear since we entered, but I had been so lost in looking for Minas and finding the stone that it was only now that I thought to comfort them as best I could.

"It's okay. It'll be okay. You're safe now."

I registered movement from the two men only a moment before the gun went off. They weren't heading for the front door or even to attack me or Ellison. They were charging the sliding glass door. The first hit it with a crash even as the second was shot, but neither of them seemed to slow down. One more blow to the glass and they were through. At first I thought they were trying to escape, but they never slowed. Instead, they hit the waist-high railing hard, tearing it free as they tumbled over and past it before falling to the ground below.

Ellison stepped out on the ruined balcony and looked down. "Fuck, I think they're dead or close to it." He glanced up at me. "Get your girls free. I need to call this in now."

I nodded and went to them, hugging them briefly before freeing their mouths and hands. They were all hugging me back, crying and asking if it was over. I lied to them and said it was. Hopefully it wasn't much of a lie. I planned to end it all soon.

Pulling back, I focused on each of them for a moment, trying to burn their faces into my memory. I wanted something good to hold onto when I was alone in the dark with that thing. "I love you all so much." I started to cry as I went on. "I know I wasn't always a good person, and you always loved me in spite of my mistakes. There may be a lot of weird things you hear in the next few days, and I know you may never understand most of this…heck, neither do I. But always know how much I love all three of you. You were always the best part of me."

Not wanting to prolong it any further, I turned to grab the stone, intending on taking it back downstairs and driving it far away from them. Find some secluded place to bury it and me, hopefully really forever this time.

But it was gone.

"Missing something, Papa?" Kristi was only four and still mumbled a lot when she talked, but this was loud and clear. The voice was hers and not hers. I felt my knees weakening as I heard its voice woven through. "Want me to help you look for it?" I turned back and saw a knowing grin on my little girl's face as it mocked me.

Sandra and Alice knew something was wrong. They were frowning at Kristi, and after a moment Alice was sliding off the bed and coming closer to me. Sandra reached out to touch Kristi's face and I moved to stop her, but I was too late. Our baby girl launched herself past the outreached hand and bit down on Sandra's face.

Blood sprayed against the wall as Alice joined her mother in screaming in terror. Ellison came back in from the balcony and dropped his phone when he saw what was happening. We both moved to pull Kristi off, but she was impossibly strong. I was yelling, but I have no idea what. I was out of my mind with anger and fear, and as I watched, the thing in Kristi was crawling up Sandra's face with its gnawing, questing mouth. It had started on her left cheek, but it quickly moved along its path of ruin to Sandra's eye. As it bit down on the interior of her eye socket, a wet crunching sound was met by Sandra's keen animal wail as she passed out. The goddamned thing was making her eat Sandra's eye.

Anger flared brighter in my chest and I planted my feet. Ellison, seeming to sense my intent, braced against the slumping Sandra as I yanked as hard as I could to pull Kristi off of her, fearing it still wouldn't be enough. Except it was more than enough. As I pulled, Kristi just let go.

We stumbled and fell past the carpet, past the broken glass door, to the end of the broken balcony. For a moment I stood on the edge, trying to tilt us back the other way, working against momentum and gravity and inevitability. And then we were floating through the air and I could feel the deep rumble from my little girl's chest as we headed for the ground. It was laughing.

It was over the next moment. Pain flared through my body and I let out a scream of agony that turned to despair as I realized I wasn't that badly hurt. I had landed on Kristi.

Dragging myself off of her, I rubbed dirt and blood off her face as I tried to wake her, to wake it. "Ask me your question. I'll answer, I'll answer!"

One of her eyes fluttered open, the other one crushed closed and tangled in a mass of welling blood. Her good eye couldn't focus, but I knew she was searching for me. "Daddy?" She looked like she was going to say something else, but then she was gone.

I screamed and cried, beating the ground and hitting myself over and over. My arm was broken, and the pain that tore through me with each blow seemed like the least of what I deserved. Why hadn't it taken me? Why hadn't it just asked its last question?

"Because the questions were never the point, my boy," Ellison was standing over me, and I saw now that Alice and Sandra were there too, forming a rough semi-circle around me and the crushed horror of our baby girl.

"I don't need the questions to take you. Never did," Alice said as it smirked at me.

"But I'm very old, and I get bored." Sandra said, "It's more fun if I spice it up. And it's easier to take the special ones like you, my long-term hosts, if you have a bit of hope and a sprinkle of mystery to go with your terror and despair."

"Ways you can fight me," Ellison said.

"Rules that can protect you," Alice added.

"Some noble sacrifice you can make to atone for being the stupid little waste that you are." Sandra's smile was thin and cold as she shoved me lightly with the toe of her shoe. "And what can I say? It makes you tastier too. Unlike the others, I'll hold off a good long time before I eat you, but what can I say? **I LIKE TO SEASON MY MEAT.**"

I had no response to give, and apparently it needed none. The world exploded as I suddenly felt an enormous pressure in my skull. I had the image of the rock appearing there, tearing and pressing at the brain tissue to make room. I knew that was impossible—I'd be dead or in a coma from something like that—but I somehow knew it was still true.

It was like Emily described. I could feel it inside me now. Sandra, Alice and Ellison all slumped to the ground like puppets with their strings cut, but when I checked them they were alive. I didn't have any way of knowing if they would ever be okay again, but then again, nothing COULD ever be okay again. I looked down at my shirt, covered in my baby's blood, and I stripped it off before running for my car.

The Gravekeeper was quiet in its new home and didn't stir as I drove away from the motel and the nearby town. I went deeper into the country for nearly an hour, searching for what might be a good spot to hide my car. When I found it, I left my car, cellphone and wallet behind, taking only a tire tool out of the trunk to use as a makeshift shovel.

I had walked for another two hours when I came upon what had likely once been some kind of large animal's burrow. It only took a bit more digging to make it large enough for me to fit inside and be out of sight. Not wanting to waste any time, I put Ellison's gun to my head and tried to pull the trigger.

Except it wouldn't let me. I cursed, I screamed, I tried using both hands, but nothing I did worked. It just sat silent, letting me try and fail over and over.

"Please just let me die. Please, please, please, PLEASE!" I knew I was growing hysterical, and I was fine with that. Maybe it couldn't prevent a natural death by stroke or heart attack as easily. I had to find a way to...

"This is it?" It was a young man's voice.

"Yes, he's in there. I thought I was going to vomit half a mile back, but it is much stronger here." This was an older, deeper voice. I was trying to decide how best to stay hidden or escape when a strong hand suddenly shot into the burrow and pulled me out. Blinking, I looked up as a large old man squatted down quickly and injected me with something. Almost immediately I felt blackness slipping in, but I still jerked when I heard the whir of an electric drill. I thought of Ellison's story and closed my eyes gratefully.

"Wait." This was the younger man again. "I can sense something about this one too."

"You can?" The older man sounded curious, but I still heard the drill drawing closer. "Interesting, but no time to risk it. Not with this one."

"No, stop." The young man again. "Don't drill him. He's different. It's different I mean. I think it wants you to drill it. I don't think it's like the others. I think it IS the seed in his head, or at least the seed is containing it somehow. Limiting it."

The electric drill came to a stop. "How could you possibly know any of that?"

I opened my eyes again and I could barely see anything. Everything was a blur. But I could hear the worry in the young man's voice. "I don't know. But I do. It's like I remember it somehow? It's weird. But we can't deal with this thing like normal."

The older man sighed. "Well, then we'll have to…" But then I fell into the black.

I'm restrained in a small warehouse basement that the young man, Jason, told me they had planned to turn into "new living quarters", but that this seemed a much more important use. They've told me what their plan is, and I can see how much the idea of it pains them. They never apologize for it, but I can tell they wish there was another way.

The older man, Dr. Barron, says they are letting me record this narrative, everything that happened from the beginning, both for their work and so that my story can be heard and remembered. I asked them how they found me, and they tell me that Ellison had called them when we were on the way to the motel. When I ask them why they aren't afraid that the Gravekeeper might take them over or use me to hurt them, they share a glance before telling me that while there are always risks, they have some "unique immunities" to these kinds of things and are experienced with such matters.

Dr. Barron lightly gripped my chin then, and it was clear he was no longer talking to me, but rather the thing nesting in my brain. "Besides, I don't think it wants to fight us. I think it's exactly where it wants to be." I saw Jason's eyebrows go up behind him.

"What? Why do you say that?"

The doctor kept hold of me, looking into my eyes as though trying to peer through and behind them to the monster. "Because from everything we've heard of this creature, it is very old and cunning. Very good at getting its way." I felt a dull thrill of fear as his face hardened. "And we may not know why yet, but we will. And when that day comes, the Gravekeeper may learn it isn't quite as smart as it likes to think."

I wish things had turned out differently. I'm scared of being alone with that thing and my only hope is that the burial carries me beyond its ability to keep me alive.

They tell me Ellison and Alice are okay, or as okay as they can be. They seem normal at least. Sandra is alive, but still in serious condition. My family will never understand what really happened, but I think that may be for the best. As bad as not knowing might be, the truth is so much worse.

I'm at the end now. Jason has stayed with me to record my story, and I hope he takes to heart what I say next. These men are good men, and I bear them no ill will. They're just doing a better job of what I already tried to do. Up above, I can hear the beeping noise of the cement truck as it approaches the edge of the subterranean room I'm in. I hope that it's enough.

So listen to me before you go, Jason. Listen, whoever hears my story. Keep me buried. Buried forever. Do not ever let the Gravekeeper out again. Please. Don't...

"We both know that's not the way this will play out, don't we, boy?" I turned off the recorder and looked down at where Mark Sullivan was chained on the floor. The voice coming out of him now was rough and hard on the ears. "We both know we'll be seeing each other again."

I thumbed the button to back the tape up to before the Gravekeeper had spoken. "Yeah, I suppose we do. Sweet dreams, you evil fuck."

Moving up the steps to the surface floor, I nodded to my grandfather's reflection in the side mirror of the truck. "Looks good, grandpa." With that, I started the flow of concrete into the room below. The thing down there was chuckling to itself, but soon the flow of liquid rock silenced it, and within ten minutes it was done.

I turned around at a hand on my shoulder and smiled at my grandfather sadly. "I really hate this."

He rubbed his mouth and puffed out a long breath. "I know. I do too. But it's the best temporary solution we have." He glanced down at the slowly hardening concrete. "Did he get to finish saying his piece?" I nodded. My grandfather studied me a moment. "Did the Gravekeeper ever come out to talk?"

I hesitated, but I didn't forget who I was talking to. He most likely already knew the answer. "At the end. Just 'I'm going to get you, my pretty' bullshit."

He shook his head. "Don't do that. We're right to be afraid of that thing. You were right when you realized it was different somehow.

Even down there, we're not done with it. It's still very dangerous."

I stuck the recorder in my pocket and suppressed a shudder as I stepped back from where Mark Sullivan and the Gravekeeper lay entombed. "Yeah, I know it is."

The Outsiders: Janie's Story

Part One

The first time I met Janie Forrester, I knew it was important. She had called a few days ago on the Jager Solutions phone line—a phone line that rarely ever rang and that I had never answered before. When I picked up, I was awkward and nervous, and that only increased when I heard her wonderful, melodic voice. I took down her information and hung up as quickly as I could, mainly out of some odd, misplaced fear of sounding foolish to her.

I had talked to my grandfather about the call and he arranged a time for her to come meet us here. That was significant in and of itself. In the past few months, there had only been two times we brought someone else here. I ended up killing one of them and the other was buried alive one building over. I suppressed a shudder at the thought of what had happened to Mark and of the thing that lay down there in that cement tomb, just waiting until it was free again. I tried not to dwell on the Gravekeeper and the weird memories...or whatever it was...that I had, but it still preoccupied me, haunting my mind from the dark corner to which it had been exiled. Maybe that's why I nearly jumped out of my chair when some unknown buzzer went off and the television shifted over to a security camera at the front gate.

Aside from Grandpa showing me how the security system worked initially, I had rarely had to mess with it, and it took me a couple of tries to find the right button for the intercom. Before I hit it, I took a moment to study the figure outside of Jager Solutions.

The woman was beautiful, with a kind of sad grace that made her look somewhat older than her age, which I guessed was early thirties at the most. Even through the filter of the security camera, her brilliantly white hair and large eyes made her seem unreal or magical in some way. And for all I knew, she was. The little bit Grandpa had told me of her and her deceased brother was definitely every bit as strange as some of the things I had seen in the last few months.

Because I knew it was Janie. I knew from the description my grandfather had given me and from her appearing on the day we were set to meet—four hours early, but still. But more than that, I knew because something in me somehow recognized her, almost as though I was seeing an old friend after a long absence. I found myself smiling as I fumbled for the intercom button.

"Janie, this is Jason. Come on in. I'll come out and meet you." She opened her mouth to respond, but then the gate was buzzing open and she pushed through to the interior of our little base. I ran upstairs to the main level of the large warehouse that housed my grandfather's "batcave" and opened the exterior door before walking out to meet her. Janie held out her hand and I took it, feeling nervous and excited at the same time.

"Hi, there. You're early. Um, it's fine, it's just...Dr. Barron, my grandfather, won't be back for a bit. We had to rent a cement truck last week and he's returning it. I...ah, yeah I'm rambling. Come on in." I could feel myself turning red and wheeled away without waiting for a response. I stopped when I heard her speaking.

"Jason, wait a minute."

I turned around and gave her a questioning look. Her eyes were dark and shining, seeming to brim with equal measures of intelligence and pain. She hadn't moved from where we initially met and I could tell something was troubling her. Then she went on.

"I don't understand what this is. What all this is." She gestured around at the three warehouses surrounded by a tall fence festooned with security cameras at regular intervals. "I expected...I don't know, some kind of real business? More people?" She gave a confused shrug before turning to me again. "And you…you just let me in? If you're in your grandfather's business, how would you not be more careful?"

She was reaching into her purse, and initially I thought it was for a phone, but with impressive speed she had a small revolver trained on me. "Which makes me think that this is some kind of trap. Maybe you got to Dr. Barron and now you're using his reputation to pull in people he was connected to? Who are you really?"

I raised my hands, not out of any real concern about getting shot, but to try and put her at ease. Hoping I was smiling in a trustworthy manner, I replied, "My name is Jason Halsey. My grandfather is Dr. Patrick Barron. This isn't some kind of trap."

The gun didn't waiver from its position pointed at my chest. "The problem is that's just what you would say, isn't it? Do you work for the House?"

I blinked at that. I knew from my brief conversation with her and what little Grandpa had said that she was connected to everything somehow, but it was still weird to hear someone else talk about the House of the Claw. Shaking my head, I gave a small laugh.

"I really don't. I've killed quite a few of them, for what that's worth." She didn't smile in return and I let out a small sigh. "Look, I get it. Good looking out and all that. But it's going to be a bit before he gets back. It's not as easy to get a cement truck on short notice as you might think, so he had to drive a ways. I don't want to stand out here for an hour and I don't want you to have to hold a gun on me that long. So what can we do to make you cool with things until he gets here?"

She seemed to consider for a moment. "If you were tied up. Tied yourself up...I'm not getting near you."

I thought about that morning in the kitchen with my grandfather, him tied to the chair as he tried to explain himself, and I felt a wave of sympathy and guilt at the memory. I could do that, but it would kind of be lying by omission, wouldn't it? Acting as though I couldn't move when I could easily break free? Shaking my head, I lowered my hands.

"Look, I could tie myself up, but it would only be to trick you. I could get out of any rope we'd have around here. Maybe any chain too. And I don't want to start off like that. Not with you, especially."

She raised her eyebrow. "What do you..."

Acting on a sudden impulse, I darted forward and snatched the gun from her hand. She gasped and recoiled, her eyes suddenly wide with fear. I paused a second to get a better grip on the gun and clench my teeth before shooting myself in the forearm. The sound of the gunshot echoed off the buildings and Janie took another step back as her eyes moved between my face and my arm. I took in a couple of deep breaths as the pain subsided and raised my arm up for her to see better.

"Why did…oh God. How are you doing that?" Her mouth went slack as the bullet hole filled in, leaving no sign of the gunshot wound. Waggling my fingers at her, I smiled.

"I heal really fast. Among other things. A…well, my grandfather would call it a collateral effect of one of our earlier adventures." I looked at her seriously. "My point in doing it was to show that you can trust me. I don't have any intention of hurting you or I already would have. And yes, I get that showing you how easily I could murder you may not seem like the best way to vouch for my character, but it's what I've got at the moment."

She surprised me by letting out a short snort of laughter. "He said you'd do that."

I raised an eyebrow. "Who said what now?"

"Dr. Barron. He told me to come early, to act like I didn't trust you. He assured me you wouldn't hurt me, and he expected that you'd hurt yourself trying to prove I didn't have to be afraid of you. 'To convince me the bear wouldn't eat me because it could have already,' as he put it." Her eyes twinkled a bit as she stepped closer to me. "It played out pretty much exactly like he said it would."

I took a step back, my face burning. Old motherfucker. I should have known he was up to something when he insisted on being the one to drive the cement truck back. "Well, fuck me, I guess. You could have told me before I shot myself."

Her face grew serious again and she shook her head. "No. Because I wanted to know if he knew you that well and I needed to see if you were really willing to put yourself through that kind of pain just to make a stranger feel more at ease." She paused, quirking an eyebrow. "It does still hurt you to get shot, right?"

I frowned at her. "Oh yeah. It hurts like a motherfucker."

She grinned at me. "Well there you go then. Now I know you better too. Can we go in now? It's hot out here."

I led her downstairs into the living quarters and felt a new flush of nervousness kick in. Irritated as I was with my grandfather at the moment, I was desperate for him to come in and save us from awkward chit-chat. But Janie didn't seem nervous at all, and as she asked me questions about our set-up down there and my history with Grandpa, I felt myself relaxing.

"How are you not more freaked out by all this?" I gestured to my fully healed arm and then the miniature compound we were in. "I know you said you know things. You know about a place called the Nightlands, right?"

She nodded. "Right. I'll save that until we're all together, but the short version of me is that me and my twin brother…" She swallowed as her face darkened slightly, "Martin…His name was Martin. He's dead now. Murdered. But that's not the point of what I'm telling, so it can wait." I had opened my mouth to say something about how sorry I was, but I closed it again. She wasn't interested in my sympathy for a person I'd never met. I could see in her face that she wanted, maybe needed, to talk to someone about something. So I stayed quiet and listened.

My brother and I, when we were young, we were left in a funeral home by accident. Something happened to us there that night. It changed us. We started seeing the world differently and would occasionally know things with no reasonable explanation for how we knew them. And while we had always been close, as many twins are, now we stayed together almost to the exclusion of others. As we grew up, we had a very happy, but solitary, life together.

The biggest reason for our separation from the world was a strange drive that had overtaken us in the months following that night we were forgotten. A puzzle that we solved together, and in doing so, unlocked a way to see into a magical new world that is known as the Nightlands. Over the years, we refined our techniques and developed quite a following. This was useful, not because we wanted the company, but because it gave us access to resources and knowledge that helped us in our work, our obsession.

Of course, we weren't the first people to discover the Nightlands. And there were those who jealously guarded any access to that Realm. Chief among our unknown enemies was the House of the Claw—a cult that I know you've had several run-ins with. The things you and your grandfather hunt...I know relatively little about them. But I know the House of the Claw well. Martin and I made it our business to learn about them after our first encounter over a decade ago.

At that time, we were nineteen and just developing a small following in a few cities around the United States. We would travel around the country, periodically hosting our gatherings, performing our rituals, offering others glimpses into the Nightlands. We were still children in many ways, and surprisingly (considering the circles we ran in), we had never had much trouble from anyone we met. It never occurred to us that something like the House existed, much less that we were being hunted by them.

We had been in Seattle for a few days when we were taken on the street and carried to an abandoned tire plant on the outskirts of the city. They had covered our heads as soon as we had been abducted, and I remember wishing they would put the cover back on when I saw where they had brought us. As much horror as I had seen...it was always with a purpose. It came with a certain beauty. But this...this was pain and terror and murder. Unreasoning, hungry violence that just liked to taste the blood and smell the rot.

The plant had once been filled with machinery—that much was clear from the scars on the concrete floor where it had all been removed and sold off long ago. What was left was a giant room with an enormous black crater in the middle, the hole filled with black water that seemed thicker than it should and cast off an oily, rainbow sheen in the glow of work lamps that had been set up to push back the darkness from the center of the room.

Out from that water, that water that I was beginning to notice was stirring and rippling occasionally as though from some unseen current, there was a tidy ring of ruined corpses stacked two to three bodies deep as it went around to encompass the entire pool. I realized with growing horror that the wall I had been propped against was actually more of the same—fresher, oozing bodies on top that were slowly pressing down and mingling with the older, mushier bodies beneath, all of it squeezing out a dozen steady streams of rotting corruption that drained back into the water it surrounded.

I didn't want to take in the details, but I suppose I had seen enough in my life by that point that it was inevitable. Against my wishes, my mind set to the task of dissecting and categorizing the state of those bodies, and what it found was strange. The people had been torn to pieces in many cases, though occasionally there would be a corpse that appeared unblemished...beyond whatever inevitable stage of decay it was in. We found out later they had been bringing the creature mainly local homeless people as well as a few children from further off. I think it was seeing an infant's face in the midst of all that death and ruin that broke me that night. I remember knowing it was dead but feeling like I could still hear it crying.

Then I realized it was Martin I was hearing. He was letting out a loud, shrieking wail unlike anything I'd ever heard from him. He had been set down and unhooded after me, and while my eyes had been drawn to the ring of bodies, his had found the answer to what was stirring beneath those foul waters.

I followed his gaze until I saw it for myself. And then Martin wasn't alone in screaming.

Part Two

There was a time, when Martin and I were first starting out on our path toward what we ultimately became, that we killed animals. We always did it humanely, and never with any great frequency, but between that and the years of cadavers that followed, I had already seen a great many wonders and horrors of the internal body by the time we found ourselves in that old tire factory, caught between a wall of the dead and the thing that was rising out of the black pool to meet us.

I mention that mainly because the first thing I thought of when I saw it was intestines. Coils upon coils of black and glistening entrails that were somehow given independent life. Perhaps that's what they were. But that's not all they were.

As these seemingly endless masses of sliding, writhing meat pushed up out of the dark water in the middle of the floor, I began to see the irregularities of the thing. There were bulges—bulges the size and rough shape of human bodies—being squeezed along the snakelike interior halls of that thing, the distended outline of a person shifting obscenely along until one of the numerous terminating points of the creature vomited it out like an unwanted bite of beef. Without hesitation, one of the men that were working for it stepped forward and drug the body away, and within moments it was added to the top of the corpse wall surrounding us.

Worse than that were the mouths. All the damn mouths. I first noticed one when it regurgitated the body—a series of hooked teeth ringed the opening at the end of that wriggling tube of meat, and I realized with a shudder that similar mouths existed on the ends of all the similar tendrils, as well as at irregular spots along the surface of its twisted, gleaming core. Occasionally, as one of the body bulges would pass near one of those smaller mouths, a black ichor that I imagined was part blood and part waste, along with whatever vileness the creature was stewing in, would push its way out between those yellowed lamprey teeth with a thick, wet gurgle that made my stomach clench.

I had stopped screaming, but only because I was so far down the well of despair that I knew there was no point. They were going to feed us to that thing. There was no chance of escape, no hope of help. I looked around and found Martin's eyes. He had grown quiet too and I knew he was thinking the same thing. We were lost.

As though to confirm what was to come, one of the men holding us approached and took a middle-aged woman from next to me and drug her to the water's edge. She and the other man that made up our quartet of sacrifice victims had been brought in separately, and both looked significantly worse for wear than Martin or I—she was bruised and battered with tape over her mouth, and the man that was further around curve of the body wall was wholly unconscious, and had what looked like a shin bone sticking out of his right leg.

The woman struggled weakly at first, but as the first questing tendrils of the monster found her, she began to thrash wildly. I remember seeing the insanity slipping over her eyes like a veil as the barbed mouth opened wide and began to swallow her whole. The man who had sacrificed her didn't pause to watch. He was already moving over to drag the unconscious man to another spot at the water's edge. He met my eyes as he stood up from depositing the sleeping body, and then he did something strange.

He winked at me.

My first reaction was a flush of anger and fear. I thought he was mocking me. The unconscious man's body was already halfway consumed, and he was letting me know I was next. But then one of the other two servants of that thing began to yell something.

"Hey! Fuck! That's Bill! That's not food! That's…"

His words were cut off as the man who had winked at me put two rounds into his chest. Without hesitating, he turned and killed the last of their trio as he was scrambling over the body wall. Except I was beginning to realize the winking man wasn't a part of their group, and likely one or both of the people he had just fed to that thing were our abductors' friends. I was no less afraid as he approached Martin and I, but I was distracted from my fear by my confusion. Then he leaned down and spoke to us.

"You may want to close your eyes for this next part. When you open them, it will either be close to over or you'll need to run. Use the low point on the wall...the place the man I just killed was coming over. Understand?" I nodded to him, and I remember even now that the thing that stood out to me the most was that he was so calm. It wasn't that he didn't seem afraid, because I could tell there was some mild apprehension in his eyes as the thing behind him began to move around more violently, perhaps finally realizing what was interrupting its feast. But he seemed so sure of what he was doing. Sure enough that he took the time to warn us and give us instructions if things somehow went wrong. As he turned back to face the monster, I felt my fear melting away.

Black tendrils with hungry snapping mouths were weaving closer and closer as the thing hefted its bulk out of the water more. The man seemed to watch it with interest as he pulled something out of his jacket—a small device with a square green button under a plastic, flip-up cap. The man flipped the cap up and quickly punched the button four times with his thumb. Before he was finished with the fourth press, dull concussive blasts began to echo from inside the creature, causing it to first shudder and then blow apart in wet rags of black meat and foul-smelling liquid. It never made a noise really, but you could hear the hiss of its flesh cooking from the inside as it flailed around in its death throes.

But then it seemed to disappear a split-second before all the work lights went out. I felt a new scream building in my throat when the greenish glow of a lightstick snapped to life above us. The man handed it to me and then gave a second to Martin before activating a third for himself. He then stepped forward towards the water's edge where a young boy lay gasping for breath.

The boy was maybe ten years old, and my first thought was that he had somehow been inside the monster and was miraculously blown free while he was still alive. But then he looked up at the man crouching over him and his face was marred by the hate and fear of a much older mind. In the ghoulish green light of the stick, he somehow looked every bit as dangerous as the thing he had replaced.

"YOU. I've heard about you. You think you will kill us all? You are wasting your time. We are the..." The boy's words were cut off as the man stood up and put his foot on the boy's neck while turning his head to the side. "What are you doing?" He rasped. "Wait, I can tell you things. Many, many things."

The man pulled out a large swiss army knife and unfolded the corkscrew as he let out a short, dry laugh. "Yes, I'm sure you can. Some of it might even be true." He gestured around at the piles of dead people encircling us. "But I think I know enough about what you are and what you do. Your time is over." He thrust the corkscrew into the side of the boy's head and began to twist viciously as the thing beneath his foot thrashed and flailed like a caught fish. I almost closed my eyes, but then I felt a small wave of force like a sonic boom through us. The boy's body was gone. Disappeared in front of our eyes and taking the man's pocket knife with it.

He looked over at me, his eyes hard but not unkind as he gave me a thin smile. "You didn't close your eyes."

I swallowed as I gave a weak nod. "I wanted to see." It was the truth. I've always wanted to see, I suppose.

The man nodded his understanding and extended his hands to us—big, strong hands that seemed to swallow ours as he led us over the obscene wall and out of that terrible place. When we were outside, I felt tears springing to my eyes. The man noticed and patted me on the shoulder.

"It's okay. It's over. That thing won't ever hurt anyone again."

On impulse I stepped forward and hugged him—this man that moments before I had been sure was going to kill us. He let out a surprised grunt and then hugged me back. Behind us, I could hear Martin's relieved laughter.

And that is how I met your grandfather, Dr. Patrick Barron.

The House of the Claw: Retribution

"You need to eat something."

I looked up at Haley's tired, worried expression and I tried to force a smile as I shook my head. "I'm not hungry. Let me get some more work done and then I'll take a break."

She sighed and sat down next to me, gently resting a hand on my forearm as I went back to looking at the computer screen. I had to be close. There had to be some kind of pattern, no matter how smart or careful the Reaper was. So far, my best idea had been to try and identify the time and location of every killing of an Ascendant or House member that could reasonably be attributed to the Reaper. That should give me a minimum age and hopefully a smaller search area if the majority of the murders were clumped together. Unfortunately, the pattern of death was spread pretty wide. Most of it was confined to the continental U.S., but there were some "Reaper deaths" in Europe and Asia over the years as well.

Then it hit me. Start with the first one in recent times, as it was likely closer to where the Reaper lived. While I couldn't say for sure that any particular death was caused by the Reaper, I had seen enough through my research to suspect the majority of the unsolved deaths we had suffered in the last forty years were the work of one group, or if Haley's fears were right, just one person. Looking back through it all, it seemed obvious that the Reaper had likely gotten his start with the killing of our group's own Ascendant, Dr. Marcus Salk.

But that was where I ran into a dead end. Marcus never shared many details of his life with us, and I didn't know much about his associates or his "victims". I could guess at some of it, but it was just that—a guess. If it was someone Marcus had known personally, someone who had somehow figured out his true nature, their motivation for killing him could be anything from ignorant moral outrage to revenge. Revenge seemed more likely to me, but there were so many unknowns. People he worked with as a doctor were also an option, but I had no real way of getting staff information that was over thirty years old from anywhere, much less a doctor's office or hospital. If only I could...

"Honey, you need to take a break now. Eat and rest. We've got the trip coming up tomorrow, and I don't want you to be exhausted." Haley was still sitting with me, and now she gave my arm a squeeze. "Please, for me."

I glared at her, hating the harsh tone in my voice when I spoke. "I'm doing this for you. For both of us, and our little girl." I pulled my arm away. "As for the meeting, Margaret Templeton can go fuck herself. She's not our boss and I don't have the time to waste going up there for whatever bureaucratic bullshit they have planned."

I saw Haley frowning out of the corner of my eye. "It's not just bullshit. Something bad happened out in California a few weeks ago. Something big. Tattersall, the old man Tattersall...he's dead. And the word I'm hearing is that Margaret is planning on taking things over now that he's out of the way. Not just Tattersall Global. The House too."

This got my attention. Turning back to her, I raised an eyebrow. "Is she insane? That's not how the House works. Just because Tattersall has a large following and shit-tons of money doesn't mean that the true believers like us will listen to shit from them. Much less the psycho crowd."

Haley nodded, her expression growing more concerned. "I know that. But she doesn't. She's already a megalomaniac, but she's also about to control the part of the House that has most of the money and resources and political power. How long do you think it'll take for her to make the House over in her image?"

I wanted to argue, but I knew she was right. It was hard for me to care about anything anymore beyond retribution for Madeline being taken from us, but some part of me knew that was short-sighted. Besides, Haley was right about something else. Tattersall did have tons of resources. Maybe they had buried their head in the sand up to now, trying to pretend that the Reaper wasn't real or couldn't touch them, but Margaret knew first-hand that wasn't the case. Maybe reminding her of her sister's death and her own wounds at the Reaper's hands would be enough to get her to see reason and give me the help I need to stop this once and for all.

The smile made it to my lips this time. "I was wrong, Haley. We need to be at that meeting."

It felt strange being in a room with so many members of the House. Looking around, I saw there were at least thirty people there, and out of those, I only recognized a handful. That was by design. This mass meeting of higher-ups and influential group leaders was against protocol and stupid. Before my girl died, I'd have been unable to sit there without saying something. But now...now all I cared about was getting what I needed from these people.

It wasn't that I didn't believe any more, because I did. If anything could have ever cemented my faith and certainty in the House's beliefs and primary cause, it was watching what my daughter Madeline could accomplish. It was just that I was coming to realize how warped that central framework of belief had become over time. We were letting in sociopaths, or as other House members called them, "the psychos", who were only there to give intricacy and dim meaning to their inherent, abominable drive to torture and slaughter people. We were handing over the reins slowly but surely to money men and soulless corporate types like Tattersall in general and Margaret Templeton in particular—people that cared more about the bottom line and gaining personal power than they did helping the human race ascend. The House has lost its way, I thought, and the first step towards finding it again needed to happen today at that meeting.

That's when Margaret stepped into the room, a man and a woman in business suits following her like well-heeled hounds. Her cold gaze swept the large space, and even from a distance I could see the scar slashed across her face like a brand. The brand I planned to use to get her on board with hunting down the Reaper once and for all. But first, there was the meeting and the speechifying. Clasping my hands impatiently, I tried to look attentive as she began to speak.

"Ladies and gentlemen, thank you for joining us today. I know such a meeting is highly irregular, but these are highly irregular times. Some of you may be aware that Wilson Tattersall, our company's founder, as well as a vital member of the House of the Claw, is dead. Brutally betrayed and murdered several weeks ago while working on one of his long-term side projects." She paused as hushed whispers passed through the room before continuing with a solemn nod. "Yes, it's terrible news. Wilson was like a father to me in many ways, and we are all less without him. But it just underlines the dangerous times that we live in and that it is more important now than ever that we are united."

An uneasy rumble began to spread through the room, but it quieted when she raised her hand. "I know, I know. This also breaks with tradition. Change is a frightening thing. But if we are going to accomplish our goal of helping this world, we need organization and resources. We will work together to attain organization, and I'm making Tattersall's resources fully available to insure we succeed."

"How'd that work out for your hotels, Marge?" It was a voice I didn't recognize on the other side of the room, and it drew a combination of gasps and laughs from the crowd. Everyone knew about Margaret's failed experiments trying to create a deadly super-virus, but I didn't know so many people thought it was as funny as I did. Maybe Margaret wasn't as well-liked or in control as I had thought.

Margaret's smile was cold as she went to respond. Before she could, I blurted out, "What about the Reaper?"

There was no laughter this time. You could have heard a pin drop. I saw a mixture of anger and fear pass across Margaret's face before she regained control. She did better than the rest. Most of the faces I could see were clearly terrified.

"This isn't a pep rally or a Q and A session. Just an introduction to what I hope will be a fruitful meeting of the minds. We will be talking throughout the day privately, and this afternoon we'll see what kind of agreement we have reached." She looked at me, her eyes glittering dangerously. "Let's start with you." As though on command, two people came up to "escort" me.

I think the intention was to frighten me or intimidate the others if they thought about speaking up, but it didn't have the desired effect. I wasn't afraid of Margaret or her stupid company, and as I walked out of the room behind her, I saw more looks of anger and defiance than fear. I didn't think this coup was going as well as Margaret had hoped it would.

We followed her to a nearby conference room dominated by a long wood table flanked on all sides by high-backed black leather chairs. Margaret sat at one end of the table and gestured for me to sit as well. I ignored her and stood back, my arms folded.

Smirking, she gave a light shrug. "Jimmy, are we going to have a problem?"

I glanced at the two goons in the room with us. "I don't know. You're the one with enforcers following you around like we're in a mob movie. Planning on breaking my legs?"

Another smirk and she waved her hand. I heard the door open and close behind me as the others left. "Look, Jimmy, let me be frank with you. I don't care for you much. Though I don't think you're directly responsible for Barbara's death, I've always felt that the incompetence of you and your group was a contributing factor. That..."

I felt my face growing hot. "Your sister died because of the fucking Reaper. And while we're being frank, you were with her at the time." I touched my face where the scar lay on her own. "I didn't see you stopping him either."

Giving me a smile that was closer to a baring of teeth, she went on. "That mark against you aside, you do have a great deal of influence among certain factions within the House. During this period of transition, I would really value it if you were on my side. It would make my job easier, and your own group would benefit greatly as well."

I wanted to yell again, but I forced myself to stop. This was the crack I was looking for. "Ok. I'm listening. What kind of benefits or resources are we talking about?"

Margaret seemed to be considering something before she spoke. "Well, we have a new Ascendant here. Her name is Emily. She's very unique and vital to our plan going forward, but she's also a nine year-old girl. Whatever my misgivings of you and Haley, there's no denying that you are very skilled at providing for the domestic needs of upcoming Ascendants. Caregiving and the like. Even Barbara was always complimentary on that point." She tapped on the table and a screen behind her came on, showing a picture of a little red-haired girl with freckles and a large gap in her smile. "It goes without saying that this would be a joint effort. You would have to agree to some of my people being involved with security, and any field exercises would be solely under Tattersall Security's purview."

Her words were starting to fade into the periphery as I tried to sort out several conflicting thoughts and emotions. After several moments of looking at the girl's picture, I looked back to

Margaret to ask the simplest of my questions. "What is her Ascendant form?"

Margaret smiled widely. "It's something truly amazing. She's a gateway. If she knows a place or a person well, or if she has an object that belongs to someone, she can create a doorway to where they are. She can even pull herself along afterward." She leaned forward, and I could tell her excitement was genuine. "Can you imagine the potential of that? Once she's well-trained, she can give us access to nearly anywhere on the planet. Anyone. Even better, it's theorized that she can actually access the other Realms too, though it's too dangerous to test that yet. We may finally have a direct path to the Nightlands."

This all sounded so incredible. Unbelievable. Perfect. "I'll do it."

It may take time, but once I knew who the Reaper was, I'd have the perfect weapon to find him or them and end this once and for all. I debated bringing up needing resources to find the Reaper after being given a gift like this girl, but I didn't know when I would have another chance to make demands. Deciding to push my luck, I went to speak, but Margaret was already standing up from the table with a satisfied nod.

"Excellent! I knew you'd see reason. Emily is a sweet girl, and I think you'll find she's a good replacement for the Ascendant you lost recently. Once today's meetings are over, I'll..."

"What did you fucking say?"

Margaret blinked. "What?"

My vision was turning red, anger blazing so hot in my chest that I felt like I was burning up from the inside out. I had known when she started talking about Emily that part of the reason it was being offered to us was to placate us. To give us a new child to focus on. But to come out and call Madeline replaceable? It was too much. I had been holding my rage in check since entering this temple of corporate greed that morning, been trying to hide my hate for what it and Margaret represented. But that wrath was loose now, ravenous and snapping, and it wouldn't be satisfied until it had blood between its teeth.

"She wasn't a fucking puppy." I stepped forward and Margaret took a step back, her face shifting from confusion to annoyance and fear. "She was my daughter. She can't be replaced like a goddamned pet."

Margaret raised her hands. "Look, I get it. Poor choice of words. But let's be honest and clear. The last Ascendant wasn't your daughter. Emily won't be either. They're assets, valuable members of our organization that have a bigger role to play than just playing house with you and your wife. If you can't wrap your head around that, then..."

It wasn't hard to grab Margaret's skull. Her mind was sharp and relentlessly ready for combat, but her body wasn't used to fighting. So when I lunged forward and pushed my hands past her own, it was a simple thing, too quick for her to react. I caught a brief glimpse of surprise and dismay in her eyes before my thumbs were on them, pressing them into their sockets as she began to scream.

I expected someone to come in and stop me, especially with the noise she was making. But either she was even less-liked than I thought or the room was well soundproofed. She twisted and flailed against me as I bore her down to the ground, putting my full weight behind my thumbs as they drove down in their quest to crush her imperious eyes and destroy her hateful brain. The eyes gave quickly, their fluid and the accompanying blood providing more than enough lubrication to push on to the back wall of the sockets.

She had grown still, but I knew she wasn't dead yet. So I stomped on her head until I was sure she was. When I was done, I sat down next to the body, falling into a kind of stupor as I stared at the bits of Margaret slowly drying on the expensive carpet. After what felt like only a few minutes, I heard the door to the conference room open. Hearing a startled gasp I recognized, I looked up to see Haley standing there.

"Oh God. What have you done, Jimmy?"

I just shook my head. I didn't have a response. I wasn't sure why I had done it now, only that it had made me feel much better. Still, the immensity of the act hadn't fully escaped me. How was I ever going to get to the Reaper after they found out that I had murdered their leader?

Haley was beside me now, holding my face in her hands. "Listen to me. Hey, stay with me. Listen. I was coming to tell you that in the couple of hours you've been in here, the rest of us decided. Margaret's right. We do need a leader to organize us better. But not her." A brief smile flickered across her face before turning serious again. "Me. I didn't want it, but they couldn't agree on anyone else." She glanced back at Margaret's feet. "As for that...most people didn't like her, but she did have her allies. We'll say that I came in here to tell the two of you about the decision and she attacked us. Gave us no choice."

I was coming back to myself a bit more now and I looked past Haley at the ruined head of the body laying behind her. "No one is going to believe that was self-defense."

Haley sighed and nodded. "They won't, but hopefully they won't care enough to argue against it. They just need some reason for it, whether it really makes sense or not. Unless you have a better idea?"

I shook my head again. "I'm sorry. I couldn't help myself. She acted like she was a puppy." I knew I wasn't making sense, but Haley just kissed my head and nodded.

"I know, baby. Let's get you cleaned up some and go sell this thing."

It was the next day before it was done. There had been arguing and accusations, but in the end, it went surprisingly well. The next person in line for heading up Tattersall was the young woman who had been part of Margaret's entourage at the earlier meeting. Her name was Polly Brenner, and she actually seemed to hate Margaret as much as I had, in large part because Polly was firmly in the "true believer" camp like us. She had actually been one of the main champions for Haley taking on a leadership role in the House, and she assured us she would have Tattersall under her full control by the end of the next board of directors meeting.

In the meantime, we met Emily. She really was a sweet girl, and while I knew I'd never feel more than a passing affection for her, I did feel a strange kind of immediate love for what she represented. She was the future of the House in many ways, a milestone in our fulfillment of the Grand Plan. But most of all, she was the door I was going to walk through when I went to kill the Reaper.

I'd told Polly and Haley about my plan, and after some discussion they agreed. We were to take Emily home with us. Help her develop her abilities further. And when the time was right, she would take us where we needed to go.

It was late in the afternoon of the third day before we were packing up the car to head home. Polly was out in the parking lot of the corporate housing we had been staying at, talking with Haley and Emily as I loaded the last of Emily's things into the trunk. I was so wrapped up in my own thoughts that I jumped slightly when I felt a hand on my back. It was Polly.

"I've got something else for you too. Not for now, but for when Emily's ready. When we're all ready." She held up a small, clear bag that contained what looked like a black piece of plastic. Seeing my confusion, she smiled and explained.

"This was recovered from a construction site in Atlanta in 1989. I don't know if you're familiar with the incident, but it was where the Ascendant Steven Kulchek was murdered by the

Reaper." I knew about it, and I was already feeling a buzz of excitement in my ears. "Based on our analysis and a partial lot number stamped on the inside, this appears to be part of the plastic casing for a stun gun. While the gun itself wasn't found, it seems likely this broke off in the fight that led to Kulchek's death." Her face grew serious. "We could never get prints or DNA from it, but it doesn't change the fact that whoever this Reaper is, this likely belonged to them. And when the time is right, Emily may be able to use it to find them."

Polly let out a surprised gasp as I swept her up in a tearful hug. Finally. After all this time, the path had been revealed.

We're coming for you, Reaper. Your time is almost done.

People don't realize I'm a vampire.

When I was a little girl, I used to pretend I was a vampire like in the movies. I would stalk around, pretending to bite my brother with plastic vampire teeth and hissing dramatically when a shaft of sunlight fell across me. As I got a little older and was in school, I learned to hide my daydreams when I was around teachers and other children so I didn't get picked on for being weird.

But I would still go home and read books about vampires. I would creep out of bed and watch horror movies when everyone was fast asleep. And as I got older, my idea of being a vampire started to evolve and mature. I realized that plastic teeth and the ragged black cape I had used since my kindergarten Halloween party weren't going to somehow make me a vampire. I needed to look for real signs.

Allergies to silver and garlic. Real sensitivity to light. A taste for blood. A drive to kill.

And, of course, fangs.

I was eight when I killed my first animal. It was a bird that was already fluttering on the ground with a broken wing, so it didn't take much effort. And I can't say I really wanted to kill it, but I was curious if I would feel different after drinking fresh blood. But other than throwing up a couple of minutes after drinking from where I had torn the bird open, I didn't seem to have a real reaction to it. I remember crying mournfully as I wiped blood off my lips.

As I got closer to being a teenager, I continued to be preoccupied with the idea. I would draw secret pictures of a midnight land filled with monsters and magic, imagining myself flying over it on ebony wings of taut, leathery skin stretched between ancient bones that I could shape to any form on command. I'd pass between the moon and the clouds as a giant bat or prowl the inky darkness of the woods as a marauding gray wolf. I could even turn into a swarm of large black flies if I needed to make a quick escape.

Over time, I found myself becoming more and more convinced that I had some great destiny—that I WAS a vampire, but I just hadn't found the right time or action or some other trigger that would let me fully embrace my true nature. When I was twelve, I became convinced that the problem lay in my teeth.

Vampires are supposed to have fangs, right? And my canines, while slightly pointy, never seemed to get longer or sharper. I would spend hours secretly checking them in a mirror, feeling them when no one was looking. Finally, when I turned thirteen and nothing happened, I was despondent. I had decided that thirteen was a special number and was a "vampire birthday", meaning I would come into at least some of my vampiric abilities on that day.

So that night, while my parents were downstairs cleaning up from my birthday party, I was up in my bathroom, tears streaming down my face. I checked in the mirror one last time, but I knew it was no use. If I was going to start changing, I was going to have to sacrifice for it. Clear the way for the change.

I had already brought the small pair of pliers with me in anticipation of what would come next, and to my credit, I didn't scream as I pulled the two canines that I thought were blocking my fangs from coming in. But just as the second one pulled free from the root, I got woozy from the pain and stumbled, banging against the locked bathroom door. When my parents came to check on me, they were horrified. They couldn't understand that I had my reasons for doing it, and at the time I thought it was my mistake for not telling them more about what I was going through earlier.

Because in the last few years I had taken to hiding my nature from them just like I did everyone else—partially out of habit and partially because of how my parents had changed themselves. When I was 6 or 7 talking about being a vampire, they would laugh and play along, talking about what a smart girl I was and how good an imagination I had. But at some point, they had stopped laughing. Their expressions had eroded from pride and happiness to embarrassment and worry.

So I kept it to myself.

When they first sent me to what I called "the problem school" (and was actually a home for children with mental disorders), I decided that I should just be honest with them. With the people at the problem school too. Because, I reasoned, if I did a good job explaining things to them, they would understand that I wasn't crazy, just different than them. And they would be proud of me and the extraordinary creature I was becoming.

By the end of my first year at the problem school, I saw that honesty wasn't the answer. I was never going to be accepted as I was, and my best hope was to lie better, to adapt more smoothly to the human world I was being forced to live in. So I started gradually acting like I had given up my strange ideas about vampires. I let them take me to the dentist to be fitted for a partial, making sure to act contrite and ask questions about when I would be old enough to get permanent artificial teeth to replace the two I had removed.

It took time, but I was back home and in regular school before my fifteenth birthday. I was much more skilled in maintaining my façade now, and there was no one I trusted with my secret. I made a point of blending in my freshman and sophomore years of high school. By my junior year, boys were noticing me and I had figured out the games of the girls' social cliques, so it wasn't hard for my false self, my outer self, to be popular.

To everyone else, I had become ideal. I was a smart girl (but not TOO smart), and I was pretty (but not TOO pretty), and most of all, I was compliant. I did what I was told at home and school, injecting just enough mistakes and disobedience into the mix so that I wouldn't seem artificially perfect or off-putting. When I went out with boys, I would let them take just enough advantage that they would feel satisfied without doing enough to get the reputation of being a slut.

And that might sound like a terrible existence—a life full of lies and feigned mediocrity and being used—but you need to understand, none of that mattered to me. That wasn't the real me. That was just the girl the world got. And if I'm being honest, I thought she deserved every bit of it.

I had spent much of my time at the problem school, and the years since I had been back home, reading up on various systems of belief and all kinds of legends. Did you know that there are vampire legends in almost every culture? And that nearly every religion or philosophy has something that is similar in concept, even if it isn't attributed to a monster? But by the same token, there are a lot of differences between the different kinds of vampires. The American movie vampire is very limited, based almost completely on one very specific hodgepodge of European folklore—Dracula.

By the time I was a senior in high school, I had come to understand that I had been misled, wasting my time by focusing in on that cliché idea of what a vampire could be. Because where some vampires might be weak to sunlight and afraid of crosses, others might have different or fewer ways they could be hurt. And while some may drink blood to survive, others lived off of other things.

Like pain. And fear. And death.

It wasn't a hard thing to kill my parents. They weren't really my parents, you see. They belonged to that other girl, that girl that everyone loved and no one really knew or cared about. That girl was a pleaser. That girl was a whore. That girl might have cried over the idea of starting a gas leak one night when she was supposed to be staying at a friend's house. She DID cry the next morning when I let her out so the grief and surprise would seem genuine. When they told her gently that her mother had died in her sleep and her father was in critical condition at the hospital. Oh, how she screamed and wailed.

But of course, that was all an act. There's not REALLY another girl. I'm not crazy, you know. I've just become very good at compartmentalization.

Two months after my graduation, my father was back home with me looking after him. It worked out better than I ever could have hoped. Everyone would praise how brave and good and loyal I was to change his diapers and tend to his medicines. How I was earning a special place in Heaven and my mother (God rest her) would be so proud.

Meanwhile, I could do whatever I wanted to him and he was unable to tell a soul.

He lasted for nearly a year like that, and while he had come home unable to communicate more than the occasional grunt or scream, by the end he was totally insane. I can't say for sure whether I was the cause of that—I'm not a psychologist, after all.

I'm a vampire.

And I had figured out how full and fat I would feel after spending some time extracting misery and fear from that disgusting cripple.

How re-energized and powerful. Why, I felt like my true self.

That's why I went into nursing, with my specialization in hospice care. I worked hard at it, making sure my grades were nearly perfect (but not TOO perfect) and that I had no black marks on my record to keep me from getting work just where I wanted. As luck (and some kerosene) would have it, the administrative building of the problem school burned down while I was in college, taking any record of me being there right along with it.

By the time I was twenty-five, I was working for one of the top hospitals in the southeastern U.S. as a nurse in hospice care. Primarily outpatient service, I would go out periodically to the homes of people that were already expected to die. The forgotten and expendable. It gave me a chance to get to know these people, get access to their homes, and learn their routines.

It helped me figure out when I could catch them alone and show them my true self in the dark.

But then you came on as the hospice administrator. From the start, I sensed you were going to be a problem. You watched everything so closely. You called it efficiency, but it seemed more like nosiness to me. Arrogance.

Then one day, I saw you looking at me. Studying me when you thought I wouldn't notice. It reminded me of how my mother looked when she saw my face on my thirteenth birthday, streaked with tears that went from clear to pink as they mingled with the blood streaming from my still-oozing mouth.

It was a look that said 'there's something wrong with you. I don't know what, but something is very wrong.'

I can't abide that look.

That's why you're about to take all those pills. It's a clean way to go, and much faster than I'd prefer, but I can't have your death looking suspicious. A plain jane suicide will have to do. And before you think of fighting me, you need to understand that I kind of want you to. It would give me a chance to make this milquetoast suicide into a brutal simulated rape and murder.

That's what I thought. Eat them all.

The funny thing is, you could have avoided all of this. I was going to leave the hospital next month anyway. I got a great new job at the new pediatric hospital they just opened upstate, you see.

But maybe it's for the best. You're a loose end that is best tied up, and there is some consolation. At least you got to see the real me before you died.

Aren't I beautiful?

The Outsiders: The Healing Mother

"So ma'am, as I said on the phone, our organization is going around to a number of animal shelters throughout the region for a study we're conducting. One of the goals of the study is to submit a report to the state legislature that might lead to additional grants or tax subsidies for private individuals like yourself that run limited-kill or no-kill shelters." Janie smiled warmly at Mrs. Barber. "Not that I can promise the end result, but we appreciate the work you do and want to help if we can."

Serafina Barber returned the smile briefly before looking back down at the pan of potatoes she was cutting up. Janie and I had been in the woman's kitchen for less than five minutes, but I could already feel my stomach rumbling from the smell of some kind of roast in the oven. Ever since swallowing the seed, my hunger had fluctuated wildly—some times I would go a day or two without eating and at other times I'd eat north of ten thousand calories in a day. My body didn't seem to change much either way...well, not from that at least.

I was still having the dreams about the thing we had sealed below the warehouse floor. And even after all this time, I was still adjusting to my new abilities. The biggest thing was appearing normal around other people. With Grandpa, or even Janie, it didn't matter. They knew I was different and were okay with it. But if I started moving too fast or showing I was stronger than I should be...well, even slight changes could put people on edge if they perceived some kind of wrongness in me.

Janie didn't have that problem. She had a certain...regalness about her that should make people uncomfortable, but it didn't. It was like she was a kind and gracious queen in a fairytale, and her gentle voice and easy manner soothed over any nervousness that her shining white hair and delicately beautiful features might otherwise cause. Barber was answering her questions, being far more cooperative than I'd have expected given the cold look of suspicion we'd first received when she opened the door. But it was understandable. Janie was charming, and in a comforting, genuine way that made it easy to see why she and her brother had such a cult following.

I blinked at that thought. Cult following. Janie's followers *were* essentially a loosely-organized cult, right? And weren't cult leaders *supposed* to be charismatic?

I pushed the thought aside. That was petty and stupid. We were making progress here, and it wasn't because of anything *I* had done. My main contribution had been to not glower or show the small hungry flame of violence that was burning at my core, ready to flare if we were walking into a trap or Barber suddenly tried to jump us. I sometimes internally called it my "murder pilot light"—my poor attempt at making light of something that terrified me. That hunger and thrill at destroying these monsters...it worried me more than my odd diet or having become very hard to kill.

I looked back at Janie, feeling a bit of shame. I had only known her a few days, and I still had a lot to learn about what she knew and what she had done, but I didn't doubt she was a good person. She had lost a lot and seen a lot, and she was still going. Still willing to help. And even if I'd been against her coming with me on this potential hunt, now that we were in it, I was glad she was there.

"No, it's a bad idea. A really bad idea."

Dr. Barron looked at Jason and then back to me, his eyes twinkling slightly as he regarded me. "Why do you want to go?"

I shrugged. "Because I want to help and I think it'd be interesting. I told you before, I want to be more than a spectator in all this, and I have a lot to offer."

Patrick nodded, his expression thoughtful. "That's commendable, but you are helping already. The information you've provided on the House and other organizations, as well as your network of...associates...well, if that all pans out, you may have already put us in a better position than we would have ever have been without you." He glanced again at his grandson. "And Jason's objection...well, I think it's probably born out of the idea that field work is very unpredictable and potentially dangerous."

I smiled at him and nodded. "I get that, Patrick. I do. But I'm not some fragile little girl. I've seen and done plenty, and not to sound arrogant, but there are some aspects of this world that I probably understand better than the two of you. I can contribute more than just information or financial backing."

Barron's eyebrows furrowed at the mention of money. "I haven't agreed to taking any funding. I know you're quite well-off, but..."

Raising my hand, I cut in. "That's up to you. And I know I'm giving you information in a piecemeal fashion—part of that is out of necessity, but part of that is by design. I want you to have time to get to know me. To know me well enough that you realize I can be trusted and relied upon." I turned my gaze back to Jason. "Relied upon to help in your work."

Jason met my eyes for a minute before looking down. "Janie, it's not that we don't trust you. It's that I don't trust myself. I'm not that experienced myself, and I don't know how well I'd fare if it wasn't for him and my...unique situation." He glanced at Barron before looking back at me. "This Barber case...it may be nothing, but she has connections to twenty different missing persons. It could be a bad one. And I don't want to be responsible if something happened and I couldn't protect you."

I grinned at him. "Well that's easy enough to solve. I'll protect you instead."

Barber was done with her potatoes, and while Janie was winding down on her fake questionnaire, the older woman seemed more than willing to keep talking about her shelter. She said she'd love to show us the back of the house where she kept the animals. Janie glanced at me and I nodded.

"We'd love to see that Mrs. Barber. If you don't mind, Janie here will take some photos of the exterior of your property while you give me the grand tour."

The woman glanced uncertainly between us before nodding slightly. "Very well. Come on back."

She led me through a comfortably cluttered living room to a hallway that branched off to the left and the right. Turning to the right, she led me back toward the sounds of dogs barking. She glanced back at me as we went.

"I try not to get too attached to them, you know? It's hard when they're all so cute and helpless, but it's better if I try to adopt them out when I can." She chuckled. "I can't help nearly as much if I become the crazy dog or cat lady that can't afford to feed them all."

I nodded, the flame in my belly flaring as we moved deeper into the house. This was supposed to be purely a recon mission—just investigate her and see if she warranted a closer look. But even though I didn't have Grandpa's sense of when an Outsider was near, I still had my intuition. Something was up with her, I just wasn't sure...

"Here are the babies."

Barber opened the door and I felt my stomach clench in anticipation of whatever she was about to show me. An animal torture chamber? An empty room with a dog barking played on a loop? But no. It was a large, clean room filled with dog toys and five dogs, including two small puppies that came running up to the pet gate yapping when they saw us at the door.

I started laughing in spite of myself. "They...they all look like they're doing pretty good." And it was the truth. Two of the dogs, who looked to be half-grown mixed breeds, were playing a fierce game of tug-of-war with a rope toy while a white-faced golden retriever slept on a large pet bed in one corner. She saw me looking at the older dog and pointed at him.

"That's Sammy. He's my baby. Had him twenty years this July. He's not much for playing, but he likes to hangout with the kids during the day." Her face lit up as she looked at him. "He's still got a lot of life left in him."

I felt my stomach clench. This woman is supposed to have murdered twenty people? She's supposed to be a monster? Grandpa had verified the initial tip we'd received, and had even gotten close enough to her at a pet store to confirm what she was, but still...I knew it was stupid and reckless, but I wanted this resolved now. Maybe if I asked her a couple of questions I could learn enough to at least put her case on the backburner for awhile, and maybe enough to show she wasn't an Outsider after all.

Swallowing, I nodded. "Yeah, that's really old for a dog, especially a bigger one. You must take good care of him." I looked back at Barber, my mind fumbling through the best way to start. If I was going to do this, I needed to hurry. If it was going to turn ugly, I needed that to happen before Janie came and started checking on me. Licking my lips nervously, I plunged ahead. "Say, didn't you used to work for the prison system? I...ah, well, what I mean is, in our initial research for people we should contact, I think it said you worked as a corrections officer before you retired. Is that right?"

I expected a strong reaction—anger or fear or defensiveness maybe, or at least confusion at how quickly I had shifted gears in my desperation to be given a reason to leave this woman alone. Instead she just looked slightly sad as she turned back to look down at the two puppies pacing excitedly at the pet gate.

"Just don't hurt my animals, okay? Just leave them alone."

I felt my eyes widen as I began to stammer. "I...I don't know..."

She cut me off. "Look, I'm not stupid. You know how many visitors I get out here since my husband Tony died ten years ago?" Barber turned and looked at me, her eyes dark but not unkind. "Zero. Zip. Other than the mail man and the meter reader, you're about it." She sighed as she stepped away from the gate and shut the door. "You're not cops—the last one of those dudes went missing months ago, and they'd never connect it to me anyway. An old lady running a shelter taking on violent dudes half her age? Seems unlikely."

Her eyes hardened slightly. "Unless you know more about me. One of those hunters I've heard about."

I tried to keep my expression neutral. "Hunters?"

Barber's lips thinned in irritation. "Don't play coy about it. I'm not thick with anyone, but I still hear things from time to time. Someone has been going around for years killing things...killing people like me. People that are afflicted with...whatever this is." She raised her hands. "I expect you're one of those. I figured it from when I opened the door...always had a good instinct for things since the change...but I wanted to see for sure. If you weren't what I thought, I could stop worrying. If you were...well, I'm too old to fight you." Her face tightened with worry. "Just please don't hurt my babies. Just call 911 and let someone come get them."

Sighing, I leaned back against the wall.

Fuck. Was this all just some trick? Maybe, but what if she really was harmless? "Lady, I'm not going to hurt your animals. But did you have anything to do with those men going missing? The info I got says you worked at the prison during the time period when all twenty were inmates there. And they have all just vanished in the last couple of years." I gave her a weak smile. "You say you had nothing to do with it, I might just believe you and go on my way."

She shook her head. "I don't believe that, and besides, I'm not going to die a liar. I did it. I killed all of them, and a handful more besides. And while it puts me in a bad spot, it's not something I'm ashamed of."

I felt the flame gathering strength and forced it back down. "But why? Why did you do it? Could you just not help it?"

Barber laughed humorlessly. "Oh, I could have helped it. I'm not some demented killer. But I've lived long enough and seen enough bad to know that there are a lot of bad people out there. Those men that I killed…they were some of the worst I'd ever seen, and they were just turned back out into the world to kill and rape and abuse."

"When the…when the change came on me five years ago, my first thought was that I was a monster. That the Devil had gotten into me, had made me less than human. I'm ashamed to admit that I almost killed myself one time." She shook her head and went on. "But once the initial shock wore off, I started realizing that I felt the same as I had before. I still liked people well enough overall and I still loved animals."

"You always hear that animals are the best judges of character, right? Well it's true. And my babies would sniff me sometimes like something was different, but they still loved and trusted me too. Sammy would still curl up next to me in bed in Tony's old spot."

Even in the dimmer light of the hallway, I could see tears twinkling in the corner of the woman's eyes. "It was one night when we were asleep that Sammy started having the seizures. It took a week before the doctors could tell me what I already knew. He had a brain tumor and it was going to kill him. I don't know how I knew it...I guess that instinct I have now...but it was like I could feel it in his skull giving off some low, poison buzz. And more than that, I knew how I could fix it."

She looked down as she rubbed her hands together. "I killed the first of them, Brian Fallon, two nights later. I wasn't cruel about it, and it wasn't hard. When I change...well, I'm very strong. Anyway, killing him gave me something.

Some kind of energy that I was able to hold onto and pass to Sammy. The next week, he had a clean bill of health at the vet."

"After that...well, I kept having these urges to hurt people, but I could control them. Channel them. Focus them on people that I knew didn't deserve a second chance." She wiped at her eyes and gave me a small smile. "And I was able to help so many new babies. I've got a cat down the hall that had a crushed spine when it came in here. Got ran over but somehow didn't die right out. Now it's jumping around and healthy as can be." She nodded at the door we were in front of. "Those two puppies in there? Found half-dead in a rain barrel outside of a truck stop. I couldn't save their brother, but I managed to get to them in time."

I frowned. "How are you finding so many animals in bad shape like that?"

Barber shrugged. "Last couple of years, word's gotten around. No one knows how I do it, but people know I've got a knack for healing the hopeless cases. I get calls a couple of times a month, and I help when I can." She looked away. "When I have a charge built up."

"I see."

She shook her head. "I don't know that you

do, but that's okay. I know what I'm doing is wrong, even if I'm trying to make something good come from it. So if you need to kill me, I'll accept it." She lowered her gaze and seemed to be waiting for whatever came next.

I reached out and gently touched her arm. "I'm not going to hurt you." She looked up, her face a mixture of confusion and surprise. "Look, I am a...I kill things like you. But only because they're hurting people that don't deserve to be hurt. And truth is, I'm a bigger killer than you and probably most of the things I hunt. So I'm not saying I agree with what you're doing, but so long as you...keep your standards up...I don't think I'm in much of a position to judge either." I gave her an awkward smile. "Can you do that?"

Her face brightened as she began to nod. "I can. I promise. I can control it, and I'm careful who I pick."

"I hope so. If that's true, you'll never see me again."

I turned and began walking down the hall back toward the front of the house. When I turned the corner, Janie was standing there smiling at me. "So what's next?"

I glanced back where the older woman had reopened the door to talk to the dogs again.

"Nothing. This one is a bust I'm afraid." Trying to smile, I added. "Sorry your first hunt was a goose chase."

Janie looked at me a moment before leaning forward and giving me a quick hug. "No need to be sorry. I got to learn a lot." Pulling back, she met my eyes. "Let's get back to the batcave. I think it's time I finally told you two what I know about the Nightlands."

The Outsiders: Visions and Visitations

Patrick, the thing you and Jason need to realize from the start is that I don't know a lot about the Nightlands. Not really. Part of what I know comes from what Martin and I experienced over the years of doing the heart mask rituals. Some of it comes from being connected to an extensive network of people fascinated with occult knowledge and practice. And there are tidbits of information that were gained as a side effect of us learning more about the House of the Claw and its beliefs.

It may actually be easiest to start there, as that information is the sparsest and the least reliable, both because it is second or third-hand information about a deranged cult's belief system and because what I know about the House of the Claw, even after our efforts to learn as much as we could since we were abducted all those years ago, doesn't amount to very much.

The House of the Claw believes that the soul is comprised of three parts. The part you have while you're alive in this world, they call that the terrestrial soul. There is another part, in their idea of Heaven, called the key soul or the pure soul. The third part, they call that the night soul.

These people that can turn into monsters? These things that you hunt? The House practically worships them. They see them as spiritually evolved beings that have reclaimed their night soul. This is a big deal to them, because the House believes that to be complete, you have to spiritually evolve to the point that you can gain access to your night soul. Once you've done that, you no longer have to be reincarnated and can die a final time, going into an afterlife where you get your key soul and are made whole.

Sounds like a nice little religion, right? Except according to the House, you can only obtain your night soul through experiencing violence, death, and great pain through one or many lives. They see these monsters, these Ascendants, as heroes that are actually helping people through all the terrible things they do. And the House of the Claw see themselves as martyrs willing to sacrifice everything to further the spiritual evolution of the human race.

Obviously, a lot of this is crazy bullshit, but like so many things, there are bits of truth in there too. For example, the monsters clearly exist. And they have to come from somewhere, right? The somewhere is the Nightlands.

Martin and I are…we were…especially gifted at viewing things in the Nightlands through the heart mask ritual. Where most people only get a few images or a few seconds of peeking into that other place, we were able to both see and hear like we were there, often for minutes or up to an hour at a time. As we practiced, we were even able to sometimes control where the vision took us in the Nightlands and what we saw.

Understanding how important all of this was, we took detailed notes of everything. Tried to develop a sense of what and where that other world is. When we're done talking, I've got a USB drive with a copy of all that I'm going to give you as well, and you can draw your own conclusions from what we learned.

But for now, I'll tell you what I believe based on everything I've experienced and learned from sources I actually trust.

The Nightlands is not another world or dimension, at least not like you might think of it. It is actually one of seven prime Realms. I understand that, on its face, that may seem like a small or meaningless distinction, but I can assure you it is not. Another planet or dimension is going to be governed by certain rules, right? Physics, time, the sun sets in the east or whatever. Even a very chaotic dimension is governed by rules of the larger universe it is a part of, even if those rules seem inconsistent or sometimes absent.

The Realms are different. They are outside normal reality, and the only rules they follow are those defined by the Realm itself. These places could be described as both infinite and eternal, and while they frequently change, they are always...well, they ARE ALWAYS. I don't know if it's possible for them to NOT exist.

I know much less about the other Realms. I know that Hell—which yes, it is a real place—is one of them. I have heard mention of two others, The Kingdom of Dust and The Void, but I know little about either of them, and what I have heard is not good.

I say all that to give you context for what I'm about to say. The Nightlands are very real and very important, even if I don't really understand how. They are a primary part of how everything works, like light or gravity, and I can tell you from my time seeing them that they are a wonderful and terrifying place.

But it's a mistake to look at the Nightlands as a single, unified place. A piece of land, or even an entire planet. It doesn't work like that. It's more like a Rubik's cube. If you're looking into the Nightlands, you may be on a dirt path under a green sun. If you can move yourself like I can when I'm doing a viewing there, you might travel that path for five minutes and then realize you're suddenly in the middle of an abandoned city. You may turn a corner to head down an alley in that city and find yourself in a night-time ocean.

That's one…one of several reasons…why, as much as I love the Nightlands from a distance, I've never really wanted to go there in my heart of hearts. It's very hard to navigate, particularly because these endless slices of a billion worlds don't stay still relative to each other. That same alley that took you to the ocean? The next time it might take you to a desert or a cave. Or it might just be an alley.

Because the size of these places change. The way time works changes. I've been seeing into the Nightlands for most of my life, and I still always feel like I'm looking into some elaborate clockwork that I can't begin to truly understand. And that is just the land itself. There are also its inhabitants.

The Nightlands, in all its many forms, is far from a barren place. To the contrary, it's teeming with life. There are all kinds of plants and animals, and some places have vast cities that are inhabited by one form of people or another. In many ways, it is like some kind of fairy tale land. The problem with that is fairy tales are full of hidden dangers and deadly monsters.

I think the House of the Claw is right. Based on our research and observation, it seems that the monsters we see here are coming from the

Nightlands. I've actually heard accounts of people seeing the human form of an "Ascendant" sleeping in the Nightlands when the monster version of the person was over here. Maybe they swap places, I don't know.

What I know for sure is that they aren't the only, or even the most dangerous, things in that place. I've seen things...well, I've seen and heard a lot, I guess. Enough to know that it's connected to the work you're doing, and enough to know that after this, I'm done with it.

Martin and I...we trusted the wrong person. His name was Josh. He killed my brother, but it feels like he killed part of me too. The best part of me. And he did it all to get to the Nightlands— a place he didn't really understand or fully appreciate.

I don't know what has happened to him now, but I managed to find him once using the heart mask. This was shortly after I called you, Jason, and before I began making my way here. I knew it was a bad idea, but I think I wanted to find him being hunted by some creature or starving on some frozen peak. I wanted to see him suffer for what he had done.

What I saw may have been worse than anything I could have imagined for him. He was being drug by...well, I don't know how to describe those things...but he was being drug to an enormous red building, a manor I guess you'd call it. And I knew right away where he was.

There are several very powerful beings in the Nightlands. One of them is called the Baron. I get the impression that he or she or it is relatively new—new as in centuries versus millennia, if you want to try and apply those kinds of terms to a place without normal time—but the Baron has gained control of a significant portion of the Nightlands, and it is not known for being a lenient ruler.

When I saw the man who killed Martin, he was being drug into the Baron's home. After that, I...

I stopped talking as I felt a sudden change in air pressure followed by several strangers seeming to appear out of thin air in the hallway of what Jason called "the Batcave". He was already up as the men came through the door, three of them wearing bulletproof vests and carrying automatic rifles. The fourth was an older, heavyset man carrying an exhausted-looking girl in his arms. It should have softened his appearance, but the look of barely restrained rage on his face dispelled any idea that he might have good intentions, and this was only confirmed when he spoke.

"Hi there. I'm Jimmy, and we're here to collect you in the name of the House of the Claw. You can come peacefully or you can resist." He looked between Jason and Dr. Barron before his eyes landed on me. "Please resist. I've got my orders, but I'd love to burn you all to death the way you did my little girl. **I really fucking would.**"

The House of the Claw: Apotheosis

Crossing over the gateway that Emily had created with her Ascendant form was always stomach-turning, and it didn't matter that I had travelled with her during several practice runs in preparation for this day. Walking through some kind of magic gateway from one place to another just wasn't something your body got used to, I guess.

Still, I didn't know how much of my current state I could contribute to the method of transport. I was bursting with a combination of fear, anger and excitement at finally confronting the Reaper. Aside from myself and Emily, Polly had given me eight of the best trained House members she had—nine people and Emily herself were the most we'd found the girl able to get through before she had to revert to her human, terrestrial soul form. But the members were all former or current military and were loaded down with top of the line weaponry and gear. I wasn't sure what to expect, but between the team I had and the element of surprise, I felt sure we could face down whatever the Reaper threw at us.

And then we found three people—an old man and a young couple—sitting down chatting in what looked like a fancy basement rumpus room.

Is this what we had been afraid of? Surely not.

I had a second of indecision at seeing them, wondering if the shard of plastic hadn't really been from the man who had killed an Ascendant in Atlanta years ago or if Emily had somehow made a mistake despite her seemingly unerring accuracy when she had become a gateway in the past. Then the old man looked at me as the younger guy stood up and started coming forward.

It was like a switch had been flipped in both of them—faces that had been open and relaxed a moment before were now hard and filled with purpose. The young man's eyes were filled with barely restrained violence, but the older man's gaze was somehow worse. He was just watching us with interest and maybe mild surprise, as though he had just found a new bug he wanted to study.

No, we were in the right spot. These were the fuckers behind all of this, or at least some of them. As we had planned, four of the men broke off to secure the location while the other four remained with me. Their guns were already trained on the trio as I stepped forward, an exhausted Emily in my arms as I addressed them.

"Hi there. I'm Jimmy, and we're here to collect you in the name of the House of the Claw.

You can come peacefully or you can resist." I looked between the two men and then at the woman between them. "Please resist. I've got my orders, but I'd love to burn you all to death the way you did my little girl. I really fucking would."

The woman looked a bit shocked at this, but neither of the men did. They were the ones that did it, or at least knew about it. Either way, they were all either coming back with us or dying here. And I had been honest about which I preferred.

"No need for any of that." The old man was standing slowly now and seemingly with great effort. "I'm too weak to put up a fight, and they both have enough sense to know that any firefight in here would result in too many casualties." He exchanged a look with the young man, who nodded and seemed to relax a bit.

"Yeah, sure. We'll go with you. Just leave the girl, okay? She's not a part of any of this. She's only here because we made her come. She doesn't have anything to do with your beef with us."

I laughed. "Sorry, this isn't a negotiation. Anyone who's here is going with us. But just so my team doesn't unnecessarily kill anyone trying to subdue them, do you want to tell me of anyone else that's here?"

Another look between the old man and the boy. They looked similar, possibly grandfather and grandson? Not that it mattered. They'd both be dead soon enough. Still, their exchanges were troubling. They weren't panicked, and it was clear they had some plan they were attempting.

The old man cleared his throat. "No one else is here, but there are booby traps around. Your men may not come back in one piece." He pointed to the younger man. "Jason, why don't you show them where the traps are. It won't get them all, and it will only make the survivors go harder on us if their friends are dead."

Jason frowned slightly at the older man. "Are you sure?"

The old man nodded. "Don't worry. Just go with them and show them. We'll be okay here. You can take that to the bank."

I felt like I was losing control of the situation, but I didn't see a strong reason to not take the help. If they were telling the truth, it would be good to know. If it was part of some trick, it would give me all the excuse I needed to kill them on the spot rather than risk taking them back for interrogation. Polly and Haley might be mad, but they could get over it.

I pointed to two of the members. I think their names were Rick and Selina. "You two. Stay with them. If they try anything, shoot them." Pointing at Jason, I gestured for him to go to the other two men. "You go with them. If you try anything, they are going to shoot you in the head and then come back and kill these two. Understand?" I saw the man's jaw flexing angrily, but he nodded, his eyes locked on mine. "I understand."

With that, they headed up the stairs. Emily was awake enough to stand now, and as I sat her down, I debated where I should stay. It would likely be safer for her and myself down in the basement with the old man and the girl, but I wanted to see the rest of the place for myself and I didn't trust anyone else with Emily. Also, she was looking increasingly alarmed as she came back to herself. It might be that exploring the place would be less distressing for her than watching a seemingly harmless pair of people being held hostage at gun point. I understood some of this was my rationalization for wanting to see the extent of "the Reaper" for myself, but that didn't change anything. I was here to get revenge, and Emily, while a sweet little girl, wasn't my daughter. She was a tool.

So giving her a comforting smile, I took her hand and gave it a squeeze. "Let's go look around, honey."

Narrative Summary of streamed body cam footage uploaded to cloud from Tattersall Security Unit 5482. Video partially corrupted. Files from other Units were somehow wholly corrupted and irretrievable.

The camera footage from Unit 5482, Selina Abarya, shows the initial entry into the Ascendant's gateway and encounter with the suspected hostiles. 5482 and 5988 are told by HRL19 aka "Jimmy" to stay and guard the older man and younger woman. 5482 takes up a secure guarding position with AR-15 in ready posture while 5988 does a preliminary clear of the downstairs area beyond what had already been done by the recon quad.

No other hostiles are located, but 5988 does come back stating that he can't open a large metal door in the hallway. He asks the hostiles what is inside, at which point the older man waves his hand and says, "Nothing, nothing. Just storage." in a hurried and visibly nervous manner. Based upon subsequent events, it is believed this reaction was artificial and intended to pique the interest of the team members.

It was successful.

Presumably thinking they were in control of the situation, 5482 and 5988 use command tone and language to direct the hostile to the metal door with orders to open it. The woman states she doesn't know how to while the man protests, saying there's nothing there to see. That it's empty. This is obviously an implied contradiction to his earlier statement that it was "just storage", and it is this analyst's belief that this was again intentional to ensure the team members continue compelling the door's opening.

5988 again orders the door to be opened, pressing the gun against the woman's head while using command tone on the man. The old man complies, unlocking and opening the door. From the open doorway, a large metal room containing what appears to be an operating table and various apparatus is visible. The glimpse is brief before the old man starts to wail, clutching his chest and stumbling. His words are slurred, but he seems to be saying, "My heart, my heart, oh God, not now…"

The old man staggers toward 5988, appearing to be on the verge of collapse. 5988 pivots and catches him easily, but doing so moves his gun away from the female hostile. There is suddenly a grunt followed by a gurgling sound and then 5988 is sliding down the wall clutching his throat. Further study of the video and brief frames that show 5988's wounds in 5482's camera allow a limited reconstruction of what occurred.

It appears that the man utilized the pretense of falling to get within arm's reach of 5988. He then stabbed him deeply in the area of the axillary artery—one of the few areas not covered by his body armor. This wound, while not immediately fatal, provided sufficient distraction to allow him to deal a far deadlier wound to the throat approximately two seconds later. The result was that 5988 was incapacitated and dying as the old man turned on 5482.

5482 had her gun raised, but was in a poor firing position due to her reaction to the old man's sudden outcry and subsequent attack of 5988. These factors, combined with her training about firing high caliber rounds in the direction of nearby steel, appeared to be the cause of her momentary hesitation. The old man, suddenly much quicker and stronger than he had put on previously, did not suffer from any such hesitation.

He darted forward, and based on his movements and position, it appears that he struck her somewhere on her arm with whatever bladed implement he had used on her teammate. She lets out a yell of pain, and almost immediately you see her gun fall from view and hear the sound of it clattering to the floor. Then she is being pulled into the vault by the man as he tells the female hostile to get in and close the vault door behind them.

As the door begins to close, the footage cuts out, likely due to signal interference from the dense walls of the bank vault 5482 had been pulled into.

The reason for the other body cam videos being corrupted is still being investigated at this time, and thus far, location of the operation is still unknown. It appears that some frequencies in the area were being intentionally jammed by the hostiles, so our best location estimates are based only on limited satellite triangulation, placing the site of this slaughter somewhere in the Eastern U.S. This report will be updated as new information becomes available.

"What is it?"

We were standing in one of the other buildings now—another largely empty warehouse with a subterranean secret, it turned out. Jason was looking concerned for the first time, and I felt a flush of pleasure at the worry on his face. He wasn't afraid of me or the men I had brought with me, but he was afraid of whatever was buried under the recently poured concrete floor I was now standing on.

Shaking his head slightly, Jason raised his hand. "Look, you don't want to open that. We've got explosives down there. Really volatile stuff. I don't even know how to get into it. But if you start hammering away, we're all going to go up."

I let out a short laugh. "I think your grandpa, or whoever that old fuck is, is a better liar than you, son." We had met up with the other four members, and I figured the six of them could have that thing open quick enough. "Bust this open."

One of them, Marvin maybe, asked me how they were going to do it. They hadn't brought tools for that. I told them to figure it out, and after an irritated exchange of looks, they went and retrieved hammers and crowbars from the small workshop we had seen in a corner of the other building's surface level. Jason remained silent until they started breaking out chunks of concrete.

"You're all going to die if you keep at this."

I smirked at him. "So you say. Just keep in mind, if you act up, not only will we gun you down, your friends die too. All it takes is a word on my mic and they're done."

He looked at me for a long time, his eyes seeming to bore into me with an intensity that caused me to finally look away. Just then, he said, "You know, you haven't heard from those buddies of yours in awhile." I glanced back up and saw he was smiling coldly at me.

I didn't want to take the bait, but I couldn't resist doing a quick check to make sure everything was okay with the hostages in the basement. These people were so strange and self-assured, and it was making me jumpy. Clicking the button on my body mic, I asked how things were going with "the other two".

There was no response.

Worried I wasn't using the mic right, as I wasn't used to all this weird, paramilitary bullshit, I told one of the men tearing through the floor to try calling them. He did, but still no answer. I told them to send someone to go check, but then I heard Jason behind me, closer. One of the men had kept a gun trained on him while the others worked on digging out whatever was buried underneath the floor, but Jason seemed to be ignoring him now.

"I wouldn't bother with checking. They're already dead. Just like you're about to be."

He shot back toward the man aiming at him, wrenching the gun away with enough force that I saw the man's wrist and arm twist past the points of breaking as he let out a scream. Impossibly fast, Jason slammed a fist into the man's chest twice, and even through the bulletproof vest I could hear the muffled crack as his chest caved in. Within five seconds he was dead on the floor and the other men were screaming.

Except they weren't screaming because of what had happened to their friend. They had finally broken through the floor and met what was sleeping underneath. I watched in mute horror as they began writhing on the ground before growing still as life was taken from them. And I thought I could see something pushing through the rubble, but then my world exploded as my head shattered into bright shards of pain and pressure and...something...

Something was in me. Oh God, something was in my head. I could feel it. It felt cold and unclean somehow, and in the illogic of my terror, I found myself looking at Jason, the man I had wanted to hurt and kill so badly just moments before, for some kind of impossible help. But his wide-eyed expression told me he had no help to give.

I felt like I was drowning, being pushed down into the black depths of some cold, ancient lake. An inhuman, cruel place that never saw light and only bred creatures accustomed to such conditions. It was with growing horror that I realized I was being pushed farther down into the darkness of my own soul. Not the soul of a young man full of hope and ambition as he tried to find a novel approach to the doctoral thesis I never finished. Not the soul of an older man full of love for his wife and daughter, proud of his accomplishments and what the future still held.

But the dark and stagnant tides of a bitter old man who had nothing left but his grudges and a willingness to trade away the last of his humanity for a chance to wrong those who had wronged him.

And high above, seated now in the throne of my conscious mind, I could see a foul thing looking down at me. It was looking down at me and laughing a deep, raspy laugh. As I continued to drift down, I saw it look away, using my eyes to regard Jason, using my voice to speak.

"Hello, boy. Doncha think it's time we finished what we started?"

The Outsiders: The Killer Inside

There was a tinny crackle of static and then Jason's voice. The electromagnetic shielding around the vault's speakerbox only enhanced the sense that my grandson's voice was coming up from a very deep well or some shadowed corner of a distant moon. Given the circumstances, I don't know those wouldn't be preferable options.

"Are you all right, Jason? Be honest." I tried to keep the worry out of my voice, but knew I only partially succeeded. Jason's first words when he activated the speaker outside the vault had been, "The Gravekeeper is out. I'm going with him." Given that, I considered anything short of stark terror and mindless panic a feat of restraint.

"Yeah, I'm okay. It will be okay. He thinks I know things that I don't, so he's going to take me so he can question me more."

I felt anger shoving aside my worry. "Torture you, you mean. Try to get inside your head and take you over, perhaps."

A longer pause and then another crackle. I imagined that Jason's voice sounded bleaker this time. "He says yeah, so at least he's being honest. But try not to worry. I'm tough, remember? And whatever he thinks he knows about me, I don't think he knows much about you at all."

Jason was smart, very smart in fact, and he knew what he was saying was both valuable information for me and a way of testing the Gravekeeper. Seeing how it would react. We didn't have long to wait.

A crackle followed by a voice that sounded like that of the man leading the House invasion party. "Why don't you come on out and I'll get to know you better?" His tone was light, but I could still feel the anger and violence bristling from every word.

"No, I don't think so. Why don't you leave Jason here and take your freedom while you have it? It's such a lucky break getting freed like that. It seems a shame to waste it."

If I was right as to who it had taken, that was bad. If that man had enough pull in the House of the Claw to lead a party to capture us, the Gravekeeper would have more leverage and access to resources wherever he went with Jason. It would make them harder to find and harder to get Jason back.

"Oh, I think I'll be just fine. And me and your grandson go way back. I'd never forgive myself if I didn't use this chance to catch up. But don't worry. If I don't get what I want from him, I'll be coming back for you."

What was it talking about? How did it know Jason? I've known since we first buried Mark Sullivan that the whole episode troubled Jason just like it did me. Both because of what happened to that poor man and because of the thing that lay nesting in him, waiting, wanting to be set free into the world again. My grandson was right to be scared of it. But I've also had a growing sense that Jason's disquiet went beyond that. His unique intuition regarding the creature that he once described as a sort of strange memory. I've waited to push the issue, trying to give him time to either work through it or come to me on his own terms. Now I've waited too late. Now he's being taken by something I don't understand, much less know how to beat.

But no, that's not entirely true. I don't know everything, but I do know some things. I know it isn't all-powerful or all-knowing. It can be trapped and tricked. It is able to control some people, but apparently not those like myself and Jason that have been touched by a seed, and with some limits based on distance, perception, quantity, or some combination of unknown factors. We know that it seems to jump from person to person, and there seems to be some quality that makes some people more suitable as a long-term host. This is due, at least in part, to the fact that it burns through other bodies it takes quickly, causing an unnatural rotting over time.

This was most likely an unintentional and undesirable side-effect of it being in a sub-optimal body, though the same decay likely happened at a slower rate when in one of its "special hosts". That would also likely be undesirable, as having to move from body to body elevated its risk of exposure while also consuming significant time and energy as it periodically had to search for a new host. All this was based off of educated guesses and assumptions that its behavior was at least somewhat governed by something akin to human logic, but it did track with the information we had on what it had done in the past. And if that was all correct, then I did know one very important thing about the Gravekeeper.

It was a parasite.

In some ways it matched the behaviors of a helminth, though obviously it had a lot of characteristics that were closer to some form of possession than a tapeworm. Still, much like the monsters we normally dealt with, it relied on taking over a human host. The fact that it was unique and more formidable didn't change the fact that it seemed to need a human body to survive, or at least to keep from falling into dormancy again. Which gave us a small advantage.

"You sure are quiet in there. No witty comeback or stern threat? Not even any begging for your grandson's life? You see, Jason? In the end, your grandfather is just a scared old man hiding in a hole. No one is coming to save you. You're all mine."

Gritting my teeth, I triggered the speaker. "Not for long, he isn't. That body of yours? It'll be dead in 48 hours."

A pause, and then: "What are you talking about? A bold threat hiding behind a steel door. Come on out and kill me then."

"Oh, I've already killed you."

Crackle. "I'll play along. What do you mean?"

This time I didn't try to hide the grim satisfaction in my voice. "Ten years ago I encountered a creature, what we call outsiders, that had a monstrous form that produced a very potent and unique kind of poison. It was one of the things that made me finally accept that there are some things that science cannot fully explain, or at least are far beyond my ability to understand."

"The poison was tasteless and odorless. It could be distilled down into a liquid or a gas. And it included components that don't exist in nature. Things that can be quantified, but not replicated. At least not by most means."

"I saw the potential utility in this toxin and continued to work on it after the creature that had made it was long gone. I ultimately came to realize that combining the substance *back with itself* in a particular way not only didn't consume the substance, it produced more of it. I have no scientific explanation for how this process works, but after years of working with it, I know that it does, and quite reliably. It's how I've kept the air you're currently breathing flooded with the stuff for the last several months."

This time the silence was long enough I began to worry he had just left with Jason after assuming it was all a cheap ploy. But then came the crackle, followed by the man's voice. This time deeper and flatter, the voice was somehow more terrible in its weight without the slight façade of human inflection.

"Explain."

"A few months ago we had a visitor who turned out to not be our friend. I wanted to prevent similar unpleasantness in the future, or at least insure that any enemy of ours didn't last long past the visit without my mercy. I had already installed the necessary equipment years ago. It was a simple matter to turn it into a self-sufficient cycling system for mixing the poison in with our air down here." I could feel Janie's eyes boring into me, but I ignored her. I knew she was worried I was telling the truth, that I was insane and had poisoned her, but she would need to bear with me for a bit longer.

"You're lying."

"Oh, I can assure you I'm not. But I'm also not a fool or suicidal. The poison can also be manipulated very easily to produce a cure that immunizes the person from any effects and cures past exposure if received while still asymptomatic. The monster it came from actually had a gland that produced the cure naturally, but it gave me enough guidance that I was able to sort things out from there. The three of us? All inoculated, though I must apologize to my two friends for not telling them this antidote was in one of the pokes and prods I've given them in the past. My hope was it would always be an unnecessary failsafe and I didn't want to cause them needless worry."

"But you? You and any of your cohorts you've left alive out there? Well, that's an entirely different matter."

When it spoke this time, I could almost hear fear in its voice. "I may not be able to control your grandson, but I can tell by his reactions that he believes what you've said. So I will too, for the moment. What does this magic poison do?"

I cleared my throat. "I never said it was magic, just inexplicable. But as for what it does...For thirty-six hours you have no symptoms at all. Between thirty-six and thirty-eight hours you have extreme fatigue, chills, sweating, dizziness, physical weakness, pallor, abdominal cramping and joint pain. Almost like a sudden and terrible flu. And at thirty-nine hours and twelve minutes, almost down to the second from first exposure, you suffer what can best be described as simultaneous catastrophic cell death across all systems of the body." I found myself smiling slightly. "I know you're good at keeping your hosts alive, but I doubt you're going to have much luck with that."

I did turn now to look at Janie. She looked horrified. The only question was if it was merely because of what I had said, or because of the implication that it raised. But it was Jason that asked the question I was dreading.

Crackle. "So how do you know all this? Who did you experiment on to find out it takes thirty-nine hours and whatever for someone to die from this shit?"

I sighed. "I wasn't honest with you about the number of times I've encountered the House of the Claw. Over the years, I have procured a known member here and there, hoping to get information and to have a more ethical testbed for certain theories. Rest assured, it was rare that I did it, and I always made sure they were, in fact, a dangerous member of the House and not just some misguided soul on the fringes of the cult."

Jason again, his tone angrier than before. "So that makes it okay? You just snatch people up and experiment on them? What about this little girl out here? Is she going to die too?"

"Yes she is, unless that thing out there accepts my offer. I'll provide the antidote for him and the girl if he leaves here now and leaves everyone, including the girl and you, behind and unharmed. Or he can refuse, and in less than two days he'll be down to a rock sitting in a pile of liquified remains."

Gravekeeper now, his voice still strained, but more full of his old cheerful malice. "You're a hard man, gramps. If you're telling the truth. Either way, thanks but no thanks. Thirty-eight hours is a tight window, but I think I can make it work."

I triggered the intercom again, my hand trembling with both fear and rage. "This is not a bluff, you son-of-a-bitch. You're going to die without my help."

The thing uttered a harsh laugh that made the intercom pop with complaint. "Doubtful. But what you should be more worried about is what I'm going to do to your boy in the time I have left." There was a pause and then, "Girl, take us back."

I called out again over the intercom, but it was no use. I knew they were gone. I went to the wall next to the door and opened a small panel that let me unlock the vault from the inside. Unlike the method of locking it from inside, this needed to be well-hidden, but I made a point of showing it to Janie as I performed the combination to release the door. It was an attempt at regaining some of her trust, but it was hard to tell if it was able to penetrate the shroud of fear and worry that was wound tightly around the girl.

I felt a wave of sadness for her. She had already lost so much, and because of me she was losing more. She and Jason had seemed to be on the way to becoming good friends in the few weeks she had been with us, and I treasured that for both of them. She was a good person, and as I pushed open the door to reveal they were already gone, I heard her let out a short moan of despair for Jason and perhaps the little girl as well. We hadn't told her much about the Gravekeeper, but she knew enough to know how much danger they were really in.

But when I turned back to look at her, she met my eyes with a fierce determination that impressed me. I couldn't forget that all she had been through, all she had done, had made her into a very formidable woman before she ever crossed my path this second time. It gave me hope that I could still rely on her for what came next.

"Patrick, what are we going to do?"

I rubbed my mouth thoughtfully. I could try to soften it here. Ease her into the harsh realities of what I was about to undertake. But if I did that, not only was it dishonest, but it also increased the risk she might buckle at an inopportune time as she came to appreciate the magnitude of our actions. No, it was better to just be truthful from the start and see if she had the stomach for it.

"We're going to get Jason back and we're going to stop the thing that has him. Stop it for good."

She nodded, but was frowning. "But how can we stop it? It can hop between people, right? What's to stop it from just jumping to someone that isn't poisoned or keep hopping until we can't find it again?"

I wanted to look away, but I didn't. I needed to see how she took it. If she could really be of use. "It won't be able to jump to another body if there aren't any around. I'm assuming it will surround itself with minions—cult members, guards, what have you—while it interrogates Jason. But whether it's ten or ten thousand, it doesn't matter."

Janie already knew the answer, but she asked anyway. "Why doesn't it matter?"

The next words should have been the hardest, but I found they were the easiest. This would have shamed some distant past version of myself, but that realization didn't trouble me. Young Patrick had been a good but foolish man who had failed to understand the hard truths of the world. It had cost him the love of his life, and the bitterness of that loss had cost him his family for so many years since. But in recent months I had come to understand a great deal.

The value of love and family and hope. The necessity of risking loss to gain joy and fulfillment. And the true importance of the work that we do. We were going to get Jason back, yes, but we were also going to destroy the monster that took him. It and anyone who tried to stand in our way.

"Because we're going to kill them. We're going to kill them all."

In the Right Kind of Light

"It's Mr. Doyle that's doing it. The man that lives next door? He's poisoning me."

I frowned at her. Aunt Margaret's mind was going more and more as she went downhill physically, but this kind of weird paranoia was new to me. "Why do you say that?"

Her yellowed eyes shifted nervously from the nearby window to my face. "I've seen him come over in the night. He creeps up on the bed. I can feel his weight on top of me. I try to act like I'm asleep, but I'm not. I see what he really is."

Swallowing, I sat down next to her. Had someone really been messing with her? Coming in and assaulting my poor, dying aunt while she lay helpless in bed? I felt fear and anger rising in my chest. "Are you sure about this?"

Her eyebrows knitted together. "Of course I'm sure. I know I'm getting dotty, but I'm not crazy." She paused. "Not yet."

Nodding, I went on. "Okay. I believe you. So what does he do when he's on top of you?"

Margaret's chin trembled slightly as she got a distant look on her face. "His forehead opens up. Splits open like a melon. And this long arm comes out that looks like a spider's leg, only it has a hand on the end." She was clearly terrified as she remembered it, and she had to pause several seconds before going on. "The hand covers my mouth and my nose. I try to keep my mouth closed, but it doesn't matter. It drips something onto my lips and into my nose. I feel it run inside of me, poisoning me."

I leaned back and sighed, trying to decide on the best way of approaching this. "Margaret, that sounds terrible, but you think maybe it was just a dream? A really bad nightmare?"

Her lips drew into a thin line as she locked her eyes back on me. "It wasn't a dream. And it's happened several times. He's a monster, and I know it."

"But...if it always happens at night, and with all the medicine you're on..." Her eyes widened as she sat up. "No! I saw him during the day once. I was wide awake and it was before my afternoon meds. I was clear-headed. I was looking outside, watching his house, and he came into his back yard for a minute. He looked normal at first, but when he came on out to check on his roses...In the right kind of light you can see what he really is. That's why he doesn't come out much around noontime, I bet."

I patted her arm. "I understand. I believe you. Here, let me fix your tapioca and I'll go call the police about it." I watched as she ate it like an angry but obedient child. I'd been slow with the doses of poison over the last three months, but it must have built up in her system. Made her delusional. That's why I tripled the dose tonight. It should still be untraceable by the time her organs finished shutting down in the next few hours, and I wasn't up for listening to crazy monster stories, big inheritance or not.

As she fell into what would be her final sleep, I searched myself for guilt, but found none. Feeling lighter, I went home and slept a peaceful sleep of my own.

I awoke to a rough hand clasped across my mouth and lips, two burning eyes glaring at me in the dark below a black arm that protruded from the ruined flesh of an old man's head. I tried to scream, but all I did was choke on some thick, noxious liquid that was streaming down my nostrils and between my lips.

"I tried to save her. Fought off the poison best I could, but you beat me. Took her away. But that's okay. Not everything I do helps." The alien hand on my face clamped tighter as he spoke. "Some of it hurts. Quite a bit." When he took his hand away, I found I couldn't move.

"You'll have a chance to find out all about that, though. You're going to live a long time now. Alone with me. **Down in the dark.**"

The House of the Claw: Reaper

That's not my Jimmy.

The man that went with Emily to get revenge, to bring back the Reaper so we could interrogate him, punish him...that man is gone now. The one that came back...I don't know what to call him. Jimmy claims he became an Ascendant during the trip, and that certainly might be true. He is stronger now, and he has powers of some kind—when he came back, he started giving orders, and everyone close to him has obeyed without question.

They cleared the basement level except for guards and stuck Emily in one room and the young man Jimmy brought back in the other. Any ideas of a chain of command in the House or the massive Tattersall office building we're in have been abandoned where he's concerned. He commands, and they obey.

I have only talked to him twice since they came back. When he first arrived, he recognized me, but was indifferent and strange. He was handling Emily and the man roughly, and he gave me little more than a passing greeting before carrying them down to the basement. I waited a few minutes and then followed him down.

When Jimmy came out of the room that held the man, he was already dripping with his blood. He seemed untroubled by the gore, but he was clearly irritated by the interruption. Still, he did talk to me then. Told me this man was at least one of the people responsible for killing our little girl. That he was going to find out everything he knew. That he had been rewarded with Ascendency during the mission, and he saw everything very clearly now.

I asked him why Emily was being kept down there. He said it was necessary for now. She was in danger too, and he had to keep her close. That with his newfound power, being with him was the safest place for her. I wanted to ask more questions, but he had already gone back into the room. When I asked the guards in the hall to see her, they refused. When I asked Polly to make them, she gave me a frightened look. She said they wouldn't listen to her either. No one around Jimmy would listen to anyone but him.

The plan, according to her, was to just wait and see. If he truly was Ascendant, he was likely working for the good of the House's goals. If it became clear he wasn't, we could talk about what the next step should be then. A day passed without any word from the basement. Without Jimmy or Emily coming up, or any sign of what was going on down there.

I went back to Polly then. She still asked for me to be patient, but when she saw that wasn't going to cut it, she said the best she could offer for the moment was a security room that gave me live video feeds into both basement rooms. In one, Emily was curled up on a sleeping bag on the concrete floor. She wasn't asleep, and it was clear from the way she jumped occasionally that she could hear some of what was happening in the other room. And in the other room, Jimmy was tearing the young man apart.

I thought I was going to be sick as I watched him torturing the man Polly said had been identified as Jason Halsey. Even at his lowest, his angriest, Jimmy wouldn't have been capable of doing something like that. He had too tender of a heart. There had been times over the years where I worried I'd lose him, that the harsher realities of what the House does, what it HAS to do, would become too much for him. To see the man I love…or something that looked like him, at least…doing what he did…

It didn't feel like the actions of something higher than us. Something that was causing pain or death for the greater good. It seemed more like some alien thing that was enjoying itself, and I didn't think it was revenge for Madeline either. I watched for hours, horrified but unable to stop, and I only became more certain that whatever interested that thing, it had nothing to do with what I wanted or the House wanted or what my sweet Jimmy would have wanted.

I'd avoided turning on the sound for all that time, afraid that if I heard on top of seeing, I would lose whatever self-control I had left. But I had to know. I had to know what they were talking about, what this thing was after. So I found the place to turn on the audio and felt my blood run cold.

"...gonna to tell me how you did it. Even if I have to rip you apart over and over again." The voice coming from Jimmy was deep and gravelly—the sound of some terrible stranger. What was he talking about?

Jason looked up at him out of his remaining eye. "You better work fast. Your clock is running out."

Jimmy lunged forward, digging out the man's other eye. The man jerked, but didn't scream. In fact...but that was impossible. The eye that was already missing looked like it had grown back, and several of his other wounds had faded away already as well. What was he? What if he was an Ascendant too? What if Jimmy was making a mistake, or the thing inside him wasn't good after all?

Jason's head rocked back as Jimmy struck him hard across the face. Spitting out some blood, the younger man looked back up at him placidly. "The problem you have is that you can't kill me. I mean, I literally don't know if you're capable of killing me, but aside from that, if you kill me, you can't get any of the answers you clearly want. Now I'm telling you, I don't know what those answers are. So either I'm lying, in which case, you should just keep attacking me, because that's going so well for you, or I'm telling the truth, in which case, maybe you should tell me more about what the fuck you're talking about. Maybe it'll jog something loose. Because I admit, I do feel like I know you. The Gravekeeper you, not this dude you're in. But I don't know how. So why don't you try talking to me instead of just wasting your very limited time?"

Gravekeeper? What was that? And why did the guy keep talking about him having only a short amount of time? I looked back at the other screen. Emily was standing up with her ear against the wall, listening to what they were saying. She didn't need to hear any of that. I didn't care what that thing in Jimmy wanted, I needed to get her out of there.

Narrative Summary of streamed security footage uploaded to cloud from Tattersall Security Cameras 68359 and 68360

"Maybe you're stalling, boy. But you HAVE proven very...resilient to my methods so far, so I'll try your suggestion."

HRL19 aka "Jimmy" aka "the Gravekeeper" sat down a couple of feet away from where Jason Halsey ("Jason") was chained to an old copier that had been left in the room for that very purpose. The past footage had demonstrated that the Gravekeeper had a degree of physical strength, knowledge of anatomy and torture techniques, and sadism that had ostensibly been absent before the recent mission to recover or neutralize the House antagonist informally designated as "the Reaper." The next three hours, beginning with this conversation, demonstrated just how deep the recent changes apparently ran. The working theory is that this is due to a heretofore unknown form of Ascendancy, whereby the identity of the person is wholly supplanted. Going forward in this narrative, references to the Jimmy/Gravekeeper entity will be modeled to reflect this theory.

"You want to know how I know you. I know you because you are, along with your French friend, the one that trapped me..." the Gravekeeper tapped the side of Jimmy's head, "in this fucking 'rock', as your grandfather calls it." Its voice grew deeper with anger. "Trapped me in it and banished me here, to this lesser plane of being."

Jason appeared genuinely surprised at this. "How did I do that exactly? I don't remember anything like that. Plus I have no idea how to DO anything like that. Nothing you're saying makes any sense."

The Gravekeeper rocked in his chair, clearly on the verge of more violence. "I figure it is either because you are lying, you have amnesia, or…"

"It hasn't happened for me yet."

The Gravekeeper nodded. "Or that. It seems far-fetched, but it's possible. Since we came to this building, since they learned who you really are, I've had these people pull all kinds of information up on you. Birth certificate, where you went to school, places you've lived, people you've known. In all of that, there are no gaps or irregularities they can find. To listen to them, you are no different than the rest of these…cattle."

Leaning forward, he grabbed Jason's chin. "Except…you are, aren't you? And not just because of how strong and tough you are. Or the hunting that you and your grandfather waste your time on. No…" He turned Jason's head one way and then the other. "I can almost see what you really are, or what you will be." Releasing the man, he sat back with a sigh. "But you're not the one that trapped me, at least not yet."

Jason nodded. "That's what I've been telling you. So where were you banished FROM?"

The Gravekeeper shook his head. "I don't think so, boy. I know you think you're being pert, getting me to give you information and all, but I'm only going to tell you things if they benefit me. If your role in trapping and banishing me hasn't occurred for you yet, then maybe it could be prevented from happening, at least in some timelines, by me killing you. Or maybe not, cause some things is fixed while others not so much." Standing up, he clenched his fists for a moment. "Then again, if I'm about to escape this place, go back and finish my work, maybe everything worked out just like it should." He chuckled. "What do you think, boy? Should I leave you alive?"

Jason shrugged. "Hard to say. Honestly, I think your best move is to decide and then get out of here. Because you're starting to look like shit."

This affected the Gravekeeper to an unexpected degree. He moved toward the door even as sounds of commotion outside the room could be heard. There were no cameras in the hallway, but when the door is opened, a voice identified as belonging to HL1 aka "Haley" could be heard, as well as other voices, presumably belonging to guards.

At first she was demanding to see "Emily", the young Ascendant being held in the adjacent room. Then she began asking the Gravekeeper if he was all right. That he looked sick. There were sounds of a brief struggle and then the Gravekeeper ordered the guards to kill anyone else that tried to come down into the basement. Based upon ancillary reports, it has been concluded that the Gravekeeper snapped Haley's neck and threw her some distance down the hall.

The Gravekeeper then enters the room where Emily is being kept. The girl is clearly terrified of him now, but she has been trained to serve, and does not resist when he tells her to come forward. He kneels before her and tells her to touch his forehead. To try and sense the thing inside his head. Can she feel it buried deep in his brain?

She says she can.

Can she picture where that thing came from?

She nods. A strange place, she says.

He chuckles at her. It is that, he agrees. But can you open a gate there?

She trembles. She says she's not sure. She feels so bad today. So weak.

His hands flex. He tells her she must try.

Tearfully, her legs unsteady, she agrees.

And then everything flares white.

When the light dims, only the little girl is left in the room. Becoming the gateway has taken its toll, accelerating whatever illness she was already showing signs of. She collapses to the floor as loud noises are heard from nearby. A return to the room holding Jason shows the source.

He has broken free from his bonds and is swiftly battering down the door. It is uncertain due to the lack of video coverage, but it appears that he kills the four guards outside in the hallway before entering Emily's room.

He approaches the little girl and kneels down as he takes her hand. She is trying to talk, but whatever she is saying is inaudible. He squeezes her hand and leans close, whispering to her. They speak back and forth for a short time, but all too low to be intelligible to the camera. We will attempt audio enhancement during the full forensic analysis.

Then the girl nods and Jason gives her hand a final squeeze. He says, "Give me one second." With that, he quickly stands and wipes some of the blood from his chest onto his hand, which he then uses to write a single word on the wall. Turning back to the girl, he smiles at her. "I'm ready, Emily."

There is another flash of light.

When it subsides, Jason is gone and the girl appears to be dead. Emily's body lay still for nearly an hour before it begins shifting. Melting down into a runny puddle of sludge that pools around the clothing her inexplicable decomposition has left behind. The only other sign of what has occurred in the room is the bloody word Jason has left on the wall.

NIGHTLANDS

Narrative Summary of events transpiring at TG Tower 1 and 2, as well as TG Office Alpha. Reporting completed by Tattersall Security Final Level Redundancy for archival and investigative purposes. No supplementals expected to this file.

Seven days after the abduction of Jason Halsey, five days after both he and the entity known as the Gravekeeper disappeared, an outside message began playing over all internal intercoms within the three largest publicly-held buildings of Tattersall Global. This message began playing at 11:02 a.m. EST in TG Tower 1. One hour later, it began playing in TG Tower 2. One hour after that, it began playing at TG Office Alpha. During this time, all landline phones and wired internet at these locations were also disabled, and some kind of sophisticated cellular jammers made cellular communications impossible within approximately one hundred yards of each building. This is troubling for several reasons on its own.

First, the knowledge of our offices and its systems needed to commandeer the intercoms and disable outside and inner office communication would be profound. Second, the coordination of these attacks, coupled with the sheer technical knowledge and manpower reasonably needed to accomplish it, makes the effectiveness of the assault all the more concerning. Third, the prevailing theory is currently that this was all done as a reaction to Jason Halsey being taken less than a week earlier. That means that this plan was finalized and put into action at three locations across the continental U.S. in an extremely short amount of time.

Finally, that all of this—including the unidentified, heavily-modulated voice of the speaker in the message itself—was all a mere preamble to what was to come...it is not hyperbolic to state the obvious. The implications are terrifying.

The message, in its entirety, was as follows:

Good morning. You have someone that does not belong to you. You know who I mean. If you give him back immediately, most of you will be unharmed. If you don't...

By now, you have already noticed that you don't feel very good today. That is because you have been poisoned. Not today, you understand. No, you were poisoned two days ago. You may even have some information about the poison from one of your cohorts. What I told him was true, but not wholly accurate for the strain of poison you have in two regards. First, your strain takes slightly longer to show symptoms, which is good news for you. Second, your strain can be cured up to thirty minutes before death.

Please don't mistake this for mercy. It's not. But it would be fairly useless for me to poison you to coerce you into releasing your prisoner if I didn't have a viable antidote, and it would be hard to convince you that I'm not lying if you weren't already feeling the symptoms. Fortunately, I have a great deal of experience with creating variations of the little gift that is nesting in all of your lungs. Whether that is to your benefit or your detriment...well, that is entirely up to you.

You will notice that your internet and phones are all down. But if you check, you will see that all corporate email accounts received a final email before everything went down. If you respond to that email by walking your prisoner out of one of your main buildings or bringing him to the parking lot of one of those buildings within the next hour, I will restore your communications and provide the location of enough doses of the antidote to cure at least the majority of those afflicted. Time is of the essence, as from the end of this message, you only have two hours before you will be dead— if you were at work two days ago. If you've been out this week and this is your first day back, then congratulations. You have two days to get your affairs in order.

Or you can give him back.

Chaos ensued. While there were no protocols for this, there were certain containment procedures in place to ensure no one left the building without permission. Security sealed the doors and began searching for ways of communicating. It took twenty minutes before it was discovered by one of the security staff that cell phone coverage resumed roughly three hundred feet away from Tower 1. It was another ten before the administration was notified at the other two sites. The decision was made to lock down those locations temporarily until the matter was resolved.

Then Tower 2 received the message. Then Office Alpha. During this time, it had already been determined that there was no viable response to give. Jason Halsey was clearly the person being demanded, and he had disappeared five days earlier from the basement level of Office Alpha. There were ongoing discussions about finding someone who resembled him enough to buy time and potentially lure the poisoner out into the open, but then the call came in.

Within the last ten minutes, nearly everyone inside of Tower 1 had died. Two hundred and seventy-three people had literally fallen apart into a thick liquid while another twenty-nine people looked on in horror. Presumably these people had been absent two days earlier, so they were exposed to the poison later on than their co-workers. The only reason anyone even knew about it yet was because the closed circuit relays had been turned back on so we could access the camera feeds.

Because he wanted us to see.

An hour later, Tower 2 died. Three hundred and seven gone, forty-nine soon to follow. As with Tower 1, he gave us back our eyes so we could see the carnage that had been wrought. The remaining people were fighting security, trying to get out. Ultimately, security executed those that were resisting confinement.

Evacuation was made of top leadership from Office Alpha. It made little difference. They died in helicopters and SUVs instead of their offices. Five hundred and twenty, with sixty-one soon to follow.

Ten minutes later, all cameras were lost again. In the ensuing panic, it took six more hours before recon teams were dispatched to any of the sites. There were no survivors at any of the locations. Those who had not liquefied had been shot, including the handful of remaining security forces. There were also signs of one or more individuals searching each of the buildings thoroughly. Looking for Halsey almost certainly, but also taking the time to download files, steal sensitive material, and perhaps more. The full extent of their actions is unknown at this time.

What is known is that Tattersall Global has lost eighteen percent of its workforce in one day. The House has lost its top leadership, a number of corporate members, and encrypted files pertaining to individual cells that are among the data believed to have been stolen. The three buildings have been sealed, with a controlled reporting model being utilized to account for the death toll.

This will be one of our greatest challenges in the coming weeks and months. Most of the staff had already had their personal lives pruned to the extent that they could be easily removed if the need arose. But there are over a hundred low-level staff whose deaths have to be explained and accounted for eventually. The prevailing plan is to account for thirteen percent in random manufactured "accident" narratives at various times and locations that cannot be readily contested by any family members or loved ones. These must be dispersed sufficiently that no pattern can be easily or credibly drawn. Another twenty-six percent have been identified as good candidates for a "transfer" narrative, whereby there is documentation that they were transferred to an international office, moved there, and later met some unfortunate fate in the months that follow.

The remaining sixty-one percent of this group will "die" in a chartered plane crash headed to a tropical resort for a work retreat. A fund is already being established to provide death benefits to their families and exploit the maximum PR benefit from the fund. These will be the only deaths that will be made public, and even then, they will be pulled after two days in the news cycle.

These practical measures are necessary, as they protect our interests while projecting an image of continued strength and resilience. This is, unfortunately, a stark contrast to the reality. We have lost innumerable resources and assets. We are now in a weakened position against our known competitors, such as the Kin. And we are still being hunted by this man or group known as the Reaper, with most of our primary means of learning more or retaliating being seriously degraded or entirely lost to us.

For now, all plans and projects are on hold. All but essential communication with House cells is restricted. There is only one edict, one mandate.

Survive.

The Ballad of Jacob the Beggar:
Parts Three and Four

Part Three

Joshua had been traveling for what seemed like four days when he came to the City. It wasn't a large place by some standards, but after days of wandering through a shift kaleidoscope of different landscapes with no signs of civilization, it looked like a metropolis to him. Even at a distance he could see buildings that were several stories high, and when Joshua first saw signs of movement and life, he let out a gasp that was perilously close to weeping. He picked up his pace, eyes gleaming like a man rushing toward an oasis in the desert.

Not that thirst was an issue for him. He'd not been thirsty or hungry since coming to the Nightlands, and while at first he had been grateful for the boon, in time it had only served to make him feel more disconnected and isolated from the world and his own humanity than he already did. He felt hollow and vacant, like a house that had been emptied and left bereft of any trappings or furnishings such as desire or a soul.

He still had his drive to find the creature in the Mercado Sea, and even if that waned, he had his desire to get revenge on the creature that had tricked and bound him by some strange Nightlands' magic. But those were shallow, undefined wants that rang hollow in the emptied chambers of his heart. Joshua found himself preoccupied with the idea that maybe he really had lost his soul, and with it, any real passion or wonder for the lands he was traversing.

And they were wondrous lands. In the last few days he had crossed green desert and pushed through lush groves of white trees where crystalline fruit hung like ponderous rubies that shivered and sang when touched by a breeze. He had seen a deep purple lake that seemed to freeze and melt several times as he walked around its border—all within the span of a warm afternoon.

And he had seen some signs of life at a distance—stirring bushes or a distant glimpse of movement as some animal moved here or there. Once he had even heard what sounded like a deep growl from a nearby stand of trees, and while he had picked up his pace and stayed on guard for the next hour, no attack had ever come.

But real contact, particularly with a person, had eluded him, and he'd begun to fear that was because the Nightlands was largely empty. For all he knew, there were a handful of strange creatures, himself, and the thing that called itself the Baron. He cursed his own ignorance, his own stupidity. He'd somehow allowed his passion and excitement about this hidden world to overcome his reason. Now he was bound to head west until he found the creature he sought or something got him along the way. And for what? So he could be utterly alone, walking through a magical world that he felt too dead inside to really appreciate.

But then it wasn't entirely true that he was alone, was it?

Every few minutes he found his mind drifting back to the people he'd known and betrayed. He'd see Darcy, a girl who he'd lusted after and even loved a little. A few months ago, he'd have said or done just about anything to go out on a date with her. And yes, maybe he'd known from the beginning that they weren't that compatible, but that was part of the point, wasn't it? She was different and new and exciting, and when he was with her, he felt new and exciting too.

Until that night when he first wore the Heart Mask.

He had never been particularly religious, but he felt like he'd seen the face of God that night. It was as though a small voice had leaned close to his heart and whispered the things he'd always known, or at least hoped, at his core.

There is more than this.

Magic is real.

You are special.

Was it any wonder that he loved Janie and Martin after that? They were so kind and wonderful, but more than that, they were a constant reminder of the strange new world he wanted to enter. They looked like some kind of faerie royalty out of a book, with their striking looks and their calm, refined demeanor. They treated him with respect, like he mattered.

And for a time, Joshua thought that might be enough. He could stay with them, go to their gatherings, perform the Heart Mask rituals as they prescribed and have a happy new life among his new companions and their followers. Darcy could even stay if it was alright with the Twins. He still cared about her, after all, and he knew she loved the Twins and the mysteries they represented almost as much as he did.

But then he began having trouble sleeping. His nights grew restless and when he did sleep, he had strange dreams. He would dream of being here in the Nightlands, of running across a rocky cliff toward a wide, dark blue sea. As he reached the cliff's edge, he would look down and see a shadow beneath the waves — the shadow of that wonderful creature that had sang to him a lifetime ago.

He desperately wanted to find a way down — there had to be some path to the water. If he could just make it down there and swim out, he could finally meet his friend and end what must have been a long journey. He could finally be whole.

It was at that point, as he was peering down the sheer rock face and weighing his options, that he would always hear a voice nearby. It was a coarse, old voice that seemed to carry equal measures of merriment and menace. And it always said the same thing.

"Hafta be strong, my boy. Hafta take what you want. Jump! Now, damn you! Jump!"

He would always wake up shaking and tearful, feeling so alone and afraid and filled with dark thoughts. These people weren't really his friends. Darcy didn't love him, and the Twins? They only wanted him around so long as he was useful. His ability with the Heart Mask made him an oddity for them to play with until something better came along. He needed to wake up and realize what they really were.

A means to an end.

Joshua had clung to that cold and pragmatic truth as he made his plans to enter the Nightlands. When Darcy didn't work, he moved on to Martin, and while he'd hated the thought, he knew in his heart of hearts he would have tried Janie if her brother had failed to give him the true doorway that he so desperately needed.

In the days since leaving the Baron's court, he had found himself haunted by a spectre of guilt that wore many faces. Darcy's looking confused and surprised as he attacked her, as though the idea of him hurting her in such a fashion was as alien as some of the signs he was seeing in this strange, foreign land. Martin, looking first angry and then fearful as he saw his own life fading. Martin's last feeble breaths begging him to stop it with him, to not hurt Janie.

He saw Janie, or how he imagined her, when she discovered what he had done. He knew her well enough to know that she was a kind and gentle person who held her love for Martin and their work with the Heart Ritual in the highest esteem. And now he had killed the one while forever tainting the other.

But as he drew closer to the City, the face he saw the most was his own. Josh, the guy who was maybe a bit of a pushover, maybe a bit too weak and scared for his own good at times. Josh, the guy who had never hurt a fly, much less butchered two friends while destroying the life of a third. That guy, that Josh, hated himself and hated his life, but he could at least take solace in the fact that he was trying to do good and be a good person. That even if he didn't make much of a positive impact in the world, he wasn't really making anything worse for anybody either.

The idea of everything he had done now, the changes he had undergone in just a few months...that would horrify the old Josh. He wouldn't just be ashamed or guilty, he'd be revolted. He'd call Joshua the Beggar a monster.

And he'd have been right.

It was an uncomfortable thought, and as with most ideas that differ from how one *wants* to be or act, he resisted the growing weight of it as it settled around his neck like the cord of a millstone. He didn't want to view his actions as a mistake. He didn't want to view his decisions as short-sighted and selfish. He didn't want to peer into his own heart and be revolted at the black mass he saw pulsing there.

So he tried distracting himself. Tried to appreciate the strange beauty of the Nightlands. Sought out any embers of excitement or fear and tried to breathe life into them. He even consoled himself with trying to think of ways he could get revenge on the Baron, who he half-heartedly tried to make the villain of his own story.

But it was all failing. Every step was becoming harder, as though the spectre pressing down on him was determined to push and push until his steps buried him in some deep corner of forgotten earth. And perhaps that's all he deserved, all his treachery and violence had actually earned him.

But that didn't stop him from nearly weeping with joy when he saw the City. Not just because of being so terribly lonely, but because the company he did have was so terribly honest. And perhaps he could find something or someone that could help him, or at the very least talk to him and provide some distraction from the twin voices in his head.

One was his own voice. It said things like brave and strong and sacrifice.

The other was Janie's. It said things like traitor and murderer and monster.

In time, there would be a third voice as well, but that was outside of Joshua's sight and ken as he walked into the City. He was just desperately looking ahead, and at the doors and windows as he passed, hoping to see a friendly face or a kind voice. Someone that didn't know him, and by that knowing, hate him.

So it was with both jumping surprise and overwhelming relief that he heard a light and delicate voice behind him, asking was he was lost? Did he need help? Finally, some nice woman was going to try and help him.

He turned around with a smile, only to freeze at what he saw.

The creature that had spoken to him wasn't a woman, or a person at all. She was a fox. If, that is, foxes were four feet tall, stood on their hind legs, and spoke perfect English with a refined and distinctly feminine lilt.

Joshua blinked as he backed up a step, a new thread of real fear permeating his thoughts. "Were you talking just now?"

The fox lady gave a soft laugh and nodded. "I was. I'm guessing you're not from here. Are you lost?"

He thought about different answers he could give, most of them lies. He could act confident and knowledgeable, relying on his slight insight into the Nightlands and the magical compass the Baron had buried in his skull to bluff his way along. He could act helpless and meek, as though he had no idea where he was or what he was trying to do.

Or he could tell the truth. He felt some level of fear at the idea—as though the shroud of lies was a kind of armor, and shucking it off would leave him naked and vulnerable. But then he thought of his encounter with the Baron, at what he had done to get here, and how much he had actually profited from all his sins.

So he nodded at the strange creature before him and met her eyes. "I could use some help, yeah. And I know this is the Nightlands, and I have some idea what direction I'm heading in, but yeah..." he swallowed thickly as he went on. "I think I'm lost."

Part Four

The fox that wasn't a fox had introduced herself as Tabitha, and understanding that he was lost in more ways than one, she explained that she was called a Kitsune. She said her family and many others like her lived in the city, but most of them slept during this time of day. It was only her own peculiar sleep habits that had led her to routinely walking this part of the city when it was at its most quiet.

Joshua found himself almost immediately at ease around Tabitha — she seemed to understand his ignorance without dwelling upon it, and there was an open kindness to her that made him want to trust her in spite of his attempted reserve. He asked her if the entire city was populated by Kitsunes, and she said no, gently noting that Kitsune was both the singular and plural term for her people. She said that the city was large and that parts of it frequently changed or moved, sometimes bringing different inhabitants with it. The Kitsune lived primarily in one of the oldest and most stable parts of the city, with the last shift happening before she was born. He could hear in her voice and expression that she had some mixture of pride and frustration at that fact.

It wasn't until some time later that Joshua realized the ease with which he could tell what Tabitha meant when she looked a certain way or changed her expression.   Despite the differences between talking to her and talking to a human woman, her voice and her features managed to convey a wealth of detail in every word and glance. Beyond his joy at having someone to talk to again, he felt drunk on wonder — he was talking to what seemed to be some kind of miraculous and magical creature. And beyond that, they were kind and charming and seemed perfectly willing to help him. Initially she was walking with him further into the city, but the deeper they went, the stronger his pull to veer off to the left became.   His shortest path to the Mercado Sea apparently went through the edge of the city, not into its depths.

He found himself shaking with a surprising combination of fear and dread as he slowed to a stop in the middle of a sun-dappled street. Tabitha stopped and looked back questioningly.   They had only walked together for a few minutes, but that had been enough for him to be terrified at the idea of losing the first good experience he'd had in this world since killing Martin. When she asked what was wrong, he again felt the impulse to lie.

He opened his mouth, his mind already spinning some version of things that might trick her to walk with him awhile longer, but then he met her eyes. Dark, intelligent eyes filled with both warm tranquility and shrewd curiosity. She would know if he lied, he thought, and then she might not like him any more.

Swallowing, he started over. "I...I made a mistake when I first came here. I got bound to a...a man or something called the Baron. Now I have to go to the Mercado Sea." He felt himself tearing up and wiped at his cheek with embarrassment. "I'd like to stay and talk to you, but the pull is too strong. I have to keep moving and..." Joshua pointed vaguely off to their left with a dejected tone. "I have to keep going that way."

Tabitha's face had changed slightly as he talked, but she didn't respond until he had sat quiet for several moments. When she did, her voice was still sweet and light. "I see. Well, the Mercado Sea is only a few days away if you know the right turns to make." She paused, her black nose twitching as she seemed to consider something. "I've been looking to go for a long walk for some time. If you'd like the company, I think I could use a trip to the Sea as well."

Joshua blinked in disbelief. Was this some kind of trick? He didn't know this creature, what it could do or what it might want. Why would she want to help a total stranger? He asked her this last question, and Tabitha just gave a small, foxlike shrug.

"If I helped you because you were my friend, I'd be helping because you are my friend. If I help you before we are friends, then I am just helping." She smiled widely, her long teeth flashing for a moment before she pursed her lips. "I like just helping, and if we become friends along the way, well that's good too. Then I'll be helping because you are my friend."

And that is how Joshua met the Kitsune known as Tabitha — his first friend in the Nightlands.

"The Baron is not a bad man, you know."

Joshua and Tabitha had been walking together for two days at this point, and it was the first time that either of them had brought up the subject since their first meeting. In that time, Joshua's affection for and appreciation of Tabitha's company had only grown.

They had spent hours with her telling him about the Nightlands, as well as him telling stories about his own life before coming there. She always seemed interested and curious about what he told her, but she never pressed him for more information than he wanted to give. He'd thought it might be hard to talk to her, particularly given her exotic nature, but the opposite was true.

That miraculous nature—a talking fox from a fairy tale—served as a powerful reminder of how special the Nightlands were. But more than that, Tabitha was just really cool. Not as a magic creature, but as a person...of a sort. She'd never asked him about how he came to be in the Nightlands, and if he was honest, he'd been dwelling on that and his first days there less and less as she led him down secret shortcuts and across beautiful landscapes. He could feel that they were getting closer, making much faster progress than he'd been making on his own, and a part of him felt growing unease at the idea that their journey together might soon be done.

It was that thought that was on his mind when she first said the Baron's name. He glanced over at her, confused for a moment at the non sequitur. "Huh? The Baron?"

She nodded. "Yes, you told me that you're bound because of a mistake you made with the Baron. I could tell you were angry about it. Maybe felt like you were wronged." She shrugged lightly as she glanced away. "Maybe you were, but I can tell you that the Baron isn't a bad man. He's a hero to many here."

Joshua felt his unease turning to a slow-simmering anger. "Maybe so. And...yeah, I fucked up. I tried to lie to him, and he tricked me into a spell or something because of it."

Tabitha glanced back in his direction. "Did he? Did he trick you, I mean?"

He went to answer and then shut his mouth again for a moment before responding. "No, I guess not. I didn't have to lie. He didn't make me. He just didn't tell me the consequences."

Tabitha watched him before nodding. "I can see how that'd feel unfair. Do you think the lie was the mistake, or lying without knowing what could come from it?"

He let out a laugh. "I think I might be traveling with a Kitsune therapist." When she raised a confused eyebrow, he waved it away. "No, it's a fair question. I think there was a time I would have said not knowing the consequences was the bad part. That I wasn't being treated fairly."

"And now?"

Joshua sighed. "Now...now I'm starting to think that worrying about being treated fairly instead of worrying about how I treat others — being willing to lie, or hurt people...or...or whatever, that is the bad part." Looking down at the ground before them, he added, "I don't think I deserve to be treated too fairly anyway."

Tabitha gave a rough chuckle. "It reminds me of a story my mother used to tell us as children. Hagrid the midwife." She cut a dark eye towards him. "Want to hear it?"

Smiling faintly, Joshua nodded. "Sure."

Hagrid the midwife was a large, strong woman who was renowned for her gifts with children, particularly babies. She had delivered many of the children in her town, and as they grew older, she healed them when they grew sick or got hurt. Many people loved her, and because of that love and her skill at caring for their young, they assumed that she was happy and loved them as well.

In truth, she hated everyone in the town. She had five children of her own, stairsteps from a half-grown son to a baby barely able to walk. They lived in a small but well-built house on the edge of town, and while they had meager means when it came to money, the town always made sure they had plenty of food, clothes, and firewood for the cold winter months. And every time she helped a baby be born, it was tradition that the parents would also send her home with a large roast ham and a basket full of sweetcakes.

It was during those long walks home that she would do the blackest of her hating. The ham was heavy in her satchel, the straps cutting into her shoulders with every weary step towards home. The handle of the basket chafed against her palms—cracked and red as they were from the scalding water and hours of use. But the worst part wasn't the walking or the weight of her supposed reward. It was the memories of how these other people lived.

She would be brought in like a servant, and while some of the families lived as humbly as her own, a great many of them had large, fine houses filled with beautiful things. The women wore delivery gowns finer than her best dress, and the children ran around freshly scrubbed and plump from the wealth of food that seemed to be in nearly every room.

It was the food that bothered her the most. She would smell it as soon as she walked in the door — fine soups and roasted duck, beef broth and delicate honey bread. These were things she had never eaten in her life, and for these people, it was routine. When she'd go back home with her heavily salted slab of pork and dry sweetcakes that those townsfolk likely wouldn't feed to their pets...well, it made her angry. Very angry.

Not that her children complained. They were all growing, always full of restless energy and hunger, and they'd fall on the meat and cakes like they were indulging in the finest of feasts. But then they never left home, did they? She had managed to protect them so far from how cruel the world could be. How unfair. They never suspected that with every patronizing smile, every mediocre act of charity or payment, she (and by extension, they) were being spat upon.

It was this idea that drove her to start throwing away the ham and cakes on her long journeys home. She couldn't bring herself to ask for something better—she shouldn't have to stoop to that. They should recognize her skills and talents and appreciate the fact that she had brought most of the town into the world at one point or another. Perhaps if they saw the satchels of meat and bundles of bread cast aside, they would come to realize their error.

Her children complained, of course, as that's what children do. They still had other food to eat, of course, but they were spoiled in their own way. And they were too young to understand the honor and necessity of what she was doing. That she was doing it for not only herself, but for them as well. They just had to endure, and eventually people would realize how they had wronged her. They would invite her to dine and stay with them, or perhaps even give them a fancy house in the city. These people that relied on her for so much would stop taking her for granted eventually.

The first of her children, the middle child, died the following month. Two more were gone during winter's first month, and the fourth died the following spring. The last one, the oldest, had grown so weak with malnutrition that he spent much of the time crawling across the floor of their house, half-insane with hunger and mewling for relief.

For Hagrid was still a large and hearty woman. She had made sure to sample every ham and basket of sweetcakes before throwing them into the woods. Made certain to sample the food others brought before burning them in the fire. None of them were good enough for her or her family, and she told herself she only ate what she did to see if they had finally learned their lesson. To check if they were going to reward her fairly for all she had done.

But, to her disappointment, they never did.

Her own last child had been dead a week when she went to deliver her final baby. People had taken to regarding her strangely now, and she knew that another, some young girl belonging to a family from town, was being trained in some of the things Hagrid had always done for the town. She gave the father a leering, too-wide grin as he handed her the ham and the basket of cakes, and could almost swear he shuddered as their hands briefly touched.

She thought of that shudder as she gnawed at the ham on her walk home. Her thoughts had grown stranger of late, perhaps because she lacked company at home. The deaths of her children weighed upon her after a fashion, and she marked it as another wrong against her that the town had to right. She was so preoccupied by these thoughts that she didn't notice the wolves until it was too late.

The wolves had come to the area that past winter, a large but dwindling pack that had found little game since the hard freeze had set in. It had seemed like a miracle when they first caught the scent of roast ham and sweetcakes near a path cutting through the woods. Over the next few weeks, they saw this miracle repeated several more times, always along the same road, always the same woman throwing out the food she didn't eat herself along the way.

Their pack still struggled, but they survived the winter at least in part because of Hagrid, though she had no idea at the time. And when spring came, the wolves grew strong again. They had new children of their own—hungry, yowling mouths that had to be fed. The game was more plentiful now, but it wasn't enough. And the lady with the hams…well, her trips were becoming less regular.

Perhaps that's why the wolves decided that her usefulness was almost at an end. She had one last thing to give — the meat on her own bones. The wolves fell upon her quickly, tugging her down and ripping out her throat in a handful of screaming, bloody moments. That night, they all ate well and then went to sleep contentedly, grateful for such a good day.

"Jesus. That's like a child's story here?"

Tabitha chuckled and gave a small nod. "Kitsune stories tend to be grim, but they always have a moral or two."

Joshua raised an eyebrow. "So what's the moral of this one?"

She looked over at him. "What do you think it was?"

He shrugged. "Um, I don't know." When she just kept staring at him as they walked, he looked away as he cleared his throat and went on. "Maybe don't be so preoccupied with what's fair that you forget about what's right. She killed her family and ruined her own life because she was petty and jealous and selfish." He glanced back at her. "Is that right?"

It was her turn to shrug. "Morals to stories are tricky things. Everyone can get something different from it." She smiled at him. "I like yours though."

He flushed slightly and nodded. "What moral do you get from it?"

Tabitha looked at him solemnly, her eyes glittering. "Don't be a crazy asshole or you'll get eaten by wolves."

The Outsiders: Entering the Nightlands

"Jason? Wake up. Your grandfather is here."

He had been eight years old at the time, and this marked the third time he ever met his grandfather, Dr. Patrick Barron. The first had been the night he was born, and the second had been a few months later when he'd been in the hospital with a respiratory infection. He didn't know the details of those visits, because he was too young to remember them. But even after all these years, he remembered the third visit surprisingly well.

It had provided him with a first impression of the man that his mother talked about frequently, a species of sad love typically in her voice. He knew that his grandfather was a doctor or something, and that he stayed terribly busy. Or at least that was what his mother told him when he'd asked why the man never visited the only family he had left.

There was always a nebulous and unspoken gloom that pervaded things when talk turned to Dr. Barron. It wasn't just *his* absence of course, but that of his wife, Jason's grandmother. He knew that she'd died years earlier, and while at eight he realized that was a sad thing, there was a degree of tension and apprehension surrounding the topic of her death that he didn't fully understand. But rather than make him dread his grandfather's visit, it actually made him curious. Perhaps if he met the man now that he was older, he'd come to better understand the dark thing that seemed to weigh his mother down from time to time.

It was his father waking him now, gently shaking Jason's shoulder from where he'd fallen asleep reading on his bed. It had been mid-afternoon when he had gone to his room, but today was Christmas Eve, and night had fallen hard and fast. Outside his bedroom window, the world was black and cold, and he suppressed a shiver as he sat up and put his bare feet on the cool wood floor. Standing groggily, he rubbed his eyes as he followed his father into the living room where his mother and grandfather sat talking.

The first thing that Jason remembered thinking when he saw Patrick Barron was how large the man was. Larger than him, obviously, but larger than his parents too. It was a strange thought in retrospect, because his grandfather was probably only a couple of inches taller than his father, who was himself a large but not enormous man. But there was something about his presence that made him seem bigger than that. Part of it was his physicality—he had a grace and fluidity to his movements that seemed almost alien at the time, though as Jason grew older he would come to associate it with athletes, dancers, and trained fighters he saw on t.v. Another portion was his voice—deep and rumbling, it had the strange effect of being pleasant and slightly frightening at the same time.

But mostly it was the man's eyes. His grandfather had glanced at Jason's father briefly as they entered the room, but then his eyes had settled on Jason with a weight and intensity that made it hard to breathe. They weren't mean eyes, not exactly, but they weren't normal eyes either. Normal eyes weren't so penetrating, and they didn't shine with a kind of frightening intelligence that a casual gaze made you feel as though you were being stripped down to your core. This man's did, and Jason felt his curiosity and excitement quickly shriveling up under that gaze.

Perhaps the man sensed this, because he gave the boy a smile. "Hello, Jason. You've grown up so much." A dark look flickered across his face for a moment before the smile returned. It was brief, but that was all Jason needed to finish his journey from anticipation to dread. He was starting to back up and look for a chair on the far side of the room when his grandfather suddenly fished a large silver coin out of his jacket pocket. Twirling it deftly between three fingers, he caught Jason's eye.

"Want to learn a coin trick?"

The key to a good magic trick, Jason's grandfather told him, wasn't what you hid. It was what you showed. People went into the trick with certain expectations. With a coin trick, they thought the coin was going to be hidden in the palm or the pocket or maybe even the sleeve. They may even think the coin itself was specially made so it could be folded up or concealed. And a part of them wanted to figure it out—to beat the trick and the trickster. To prove themselves up to the challenge of winning this brief contest between performer and audience.

But another part? A deeper and often more powerful part?

They wanted to feel wonder. They wanted to see tricks they couldn't crack and mysteries they couldn't explain. They wanted magic.

The key to a good magic trick, Jason's grandfather told him, wasn't tricking someone. The feeling that someone had tricked you, essentially lied to you, was rarely satisfying, even if it was all in good fun. No, the key to a good magic trick was in being open and honest with what you showed. It was in understanding what your audience wanted.

And then giving them what they needed to

trick themselves.

When Jason agreed to go with the Gravekeeper back to the House of the Claw, it was largely to get it away from his grandfather and Janie. But that wasn't the only reason. It was also because they didn't know how to beat this new monster, not really. He might could incapacitate it, trap it back underground or in a cage, but for how long? How long before it figured out a way to get free or fate sent some new bolt of lightning to split its prison in two?

Jason had always been skeptical when it came to fate. The thought that some things were just destined to be rankled his belief in free will and self-determination. But after his time with his grandfather and all he had seen and learned...well, he had a new appreciation for how little he knew. And when it came to the Gravekeeper in particular, his sense of connection and shared history with the foul thing spoke to yet another thing he didn't fully understand.

He'd been considering the idea that somehow, bizarre as it sounded to him, some future version of himself had interacted with the Gravekeeper. In many ways it seemed to make little sense—the fanciful thoughts of a kid who grew up reading too many science fiction and fantasy books. But in one way, it made all the sense in the world.

Because it felt right.

Ever since swallowing the seed, Jason had felt like he was riding through a strange land on a journey that never ended. His body was changing, he was having strange thoughts and impulses, and he had this...instinct or conviction about some things that he'd never had before. It was a small and subtle thing, and if he tried to look at it directly, it would invariably fade away under his gaze. But then it'd be back, nodding at the edge of his mind's eye when he was going in the right direction. Not telling him where he was going, but only that this was the way. He'd known it at the rave in the desert, he'd known it when he met Janie, and he knew it when he met the gaze of the thing staring out from that dead man's eyes.

So he went, knowing he'd be tortured and interrogated, but hoping that between time with the Gravekeeper and any information his interrogation gave away, he would learn something that was useful. A way to kill it or get rid of it, or at the very least, some better understanding of what was happening to him. And hopefully, if he played it just right, he could get the nasty creature to trick itself.

And it had worked, after a fashion. The

Gravekeeper was very sly, and it guarded every word carefully, but by necessity it told him enough to fill in some blanks. And with every blank that was filled in, new doors opened in his mind. Wispy, dream-like recollections that were more like shadows or ghosts than true memories. It wasn't much, but it was enough to make his new instinct stronger and more sure, and his growing certainty that he was on the right path made everything easier to endure.

The torture wasn't the hard part. While Jason still felt pain, his connection to it and its ability to overpower his mind was different and lesser than it had been when he was fully human. The mutilation and cruelty was still distracting, but with effort he could make it more like background noise while he tried to concentrate on solving the problems at hand.

At times he even wished it was more of a distraction. Try as he might, he kept coming back to the fact that he would almost certainly never see his grandfather or his new friend again. At best, he might figure out a way to stop this monster, but even if he did and somehow managed to survive accomplishing the task, what were the odds that he'd make it out of the House's stronghold without being killed or recaptured? He wasn't sure what it would take to physically stop him, but there was bound to be a limit.

Even if he got free though, could he really risk seeking them out? Jason couldn't say for sure, but he almost got the impression that the House didn't really know who the three of them were or where the little girl had teleported them to when the ambush squad showed up in the Batcave. That was lucky, but that luck would only last so long. They'd figure out who he was, and after that, it was a short trip to figuring out that his grandfather, Dr. Patrick Barron, was the other "Reaper" they were looking for.

No, his best bet was to try and find a way to stop the Gravekeeper and then do his best to destroy everyone and everything in this place. It might not stop the House from hunting his grandfather and Janie forever, but at the very least it should slow them down. Maybe he really couldn't die, or maybe he could at least catch them by surprise long enough that he could get rid of any evidence connecting him to the others before they finished him.

Either way, stopping the thing that was currently plucking out his eye was the main priority. He felt like he still only had a dim outline of what this monster was or how dangerous it may be, but he knew it posed a much greater threat than the House or a normal Outsider. And the more he "remembered", the more worried he became, particularly because he knew he was running out of time. His grandfather hadn't been lying about the poison, and despite the creature's continued strength and vigor, its stolen body looked on the edge of decomposition. He needed to move this along. Raising his head, Jason realized he could barely see out of his one good eye for the dried blood caked there. Blinking, he did his best to meet the Gravekeeper's gaze as he spoke.

"You better work fast. Your clock is running out."

Jason wished he could save the poor little girl lying on the ground before him, but he couldn't. He knew her name was Emily, and he hated that she had gotten drawn into this nightmare, but there wasn't time to get her help or even console her for all she had been through. This was because the Gravekeeper had already gone, and his only hope of following and somehow stopping it lay with this abused, terrified little girl.

And any moment she would be dead.

Kneeling down beside her, Jason gently took her hand. She was trying to speak, but he had to lean forward to catch the words.

"...sorry for what he did to you. ...didn't know..."

Jason felt tears spring up in his eyes as he

gave her hand a squeeze. Leaning down closer, he whispered, "Don't you worry, baby. It's not your fault. But that thing inside that man is bad. I need to stop it. Did you send him somewhere?"

"Yeah. Fairy-tale...fairy land."

He felt a small tug at his core. This was it. This was the path he needed. Or at least it was close. "Can...can you send me there too?"

Emily, who had been staring off before, rolled her eyes to meet his own. There was a terrible moment of unspoken understanding between them. She knew the act of creating another portal would kill her, but she also knew she was going to die anyway. The girl held his gaze for a moment before nodding weakly.

Jason swallowed, his breath growing quick and shallow. This last piece was the part he was least sure of, but it also might be the most important. When they had first come through the portal back to the House headquarters or Tattersall or whatever they wanted to call this place, a man on this side had commented how quickly they were back. He couldn't be sure, but he had the sense that to the people in this building, "Jimmy", Emily, and the squad they brought with them had only been gone a few minutes. Yet he was pretty positive they had all been at Jager for well over an hour.

"Emily? Can you send me back to the same place you sent him, but earlier? Earlier in time?"

She looked back at him, her eyes seeming to focus for a moment before drifting off again. "M-maybe. I can sometimes." Emily's expression grew more worried. "But...I-I can't control it good."

"That's okay, baby. Just do the best you can. Send me back before the Gravekeeper...uh, before Jimmy gets there, okay? Will you try and do that?"

Another weak nod. Jason was about to ask her to create the gateway when something struck him. He was about to go to a place he could only guess was the Nightlands, and he knew of no way to come back even if he succeeded. No way to let his grandfather know that he was still alive and that he had left because he was trying to make things better.

Jason had always loved his parents and been proud of them, but he'd never been especially proud of himself. Not until he'd found his new life with his grandfather. The idea of Dr. Barron finding that place, which he inevitably would, and seeing nothing but signs of Jason's torture and failure...it was a thought he couldn't bear. Both because he didn't want the old man to worry, but also because he wanted his grandfather to know he'd made the right choice in letting Jason stay and help fight against the Outsiders and the House. He wanted his grandpa to not feel guilty for how things had turned out, and instead be proud of the man that Jason had become.

He glanced at the back wall before looking down at the little girl again. "You ready?" When she nodded, he gave her hand one last squeeze before rising. "Give me one second."

Using the blood that coated him, some his and some not, he wrote a single word in large letters across the wall. *NIGHTLANDS.* He then turned back to the dying girl, giving her a final, sad smile.

"I'm ready, Emily."

There was a bright flash of light, and then he was...

In the Nightlands.

He felt a moment of vertigo as he felt himself falling into a puff of fine, black sand. It was as though he'd entered this new world halfway between standing and falling, and if not for his unnatural speed, he likely would have wound up with a face full of dirt instead of catching himself an inch above it. Standing back up, he brushed the sand from his palms and looked around. No sign of the Gravekeeper or anyone else, and the sand around him looked undisturbed.

He was on a beach of some kind, though he didn't appear to be at an ocean or even an inlet of some smaller sea. Rather he had the sense he was on the edge of some massive lake, and at the bounds of his vision he thought he could see tall trees sheltering a cove on the far side. The lake itself looked cold despite the warm sun that was...wait a minute.

It was bright as the middle of the day, and he could see the faint outline of his own shadow curled around his feet, but when he looked into the sky, there was no sun. And not because the sky wasn't clear—while it carried an odd purplish-blue hue, the few wisps of white cloud weren't enough to hide anything, and overall the air tasted clean and clear. It reminded him of the air quality up in the mountains, but even more pronounced, and it certainly wasn't hazy or otherwise limiting visibility. And yet there was no sun to be found.

Shaking his head, he had to remind himself that the lack of a visible light source was the least of the strange things he'd likely encounter here. Based on what Janie had told them, the Nightlands was an ever-shifting and dangerous place filled with various creatures both wonderful and terrible. He had a definite advantage given his abilities, and if he managed to find and kill the Gravekeeper somehow, he might actually live for a good while here before something got him. So the sooner he got over being shocked at every weird thing he saw here, the better.

Squinting, he looked again around the edges of the lake he could make out from his spot on the beach. He saw no signs of habitation—no docks or houses or boats—but he was also seeing a relatively small portion of a large lake. Besides, if Janie was right, the Nightlands was well-populated by...various things, but it was also massive and ever-changing. So it might be some time before he ran into anyone, much less someone or something he could communicate with.

Movement suddenly caught his eye out on the placid surface of the lake. Just a quick swirl of water two hundred feet or more away from the shore, but large enough that it implied something massive shifting down in those dark depths. He'd been considering washing off some of the blood he was covered in, but going into that was a big fuck no.

Keeping the lake in his peripheral vision, Jason started moving up the black sand beach, slowly heading away from the water and up a hill where the fine dirt turned to reddish clay and then to hard packed dirt and scrub grass. He was heading into a large flat grassland, blades of yellow and red mixed in with the light green he was used to. He was trying to keep his guard up, but his precaution was constantly at war with his sense of wonder. It really was a magical place, and being here made it easier to see why Janie both loved and feared it as she did.

He let out a gasp as cold rain lashed his face. Blinking, he saw that his surroundings had changed to the peak of a hill in the middle of a freezing rainstorm. Turning back to look the way he had come, he saw no sign of the temperate grassland he'd been walking through only a second before.

"Fuck me."

For not the first or the last time, he felt a dull sense of unreality and panic trying to crawl up the back of his skull and consume his control and his reason. This place was so alien and illogical. How could he ever hope to survive, much less find the Gravekeeper here? All he had done was condemn himself to dying alone in a strange place.

But no. He couldn't think like that. This wasn't just about him. He wasn't just Jason Halsey, dude who was a nice guy and just wanted to go along to get along. He was the grandson of Dr. Patrick fucking Barron, the closest thing to a superhero he'd ever seen in real life. A man who had dedicated his life to hunting monsters and helping people, and who had accomplished miracles through his intellect and sheer will.

Now here he was, with all the abilities he had, all the things his grandfather had taught him in the last few months, and he was going to cry about a little bit of rain? About being lost? Fuck that. He wouldn't melt, and he could already feel that vague sense of heading in the right direction whispering from the back of his mind. But even without that, it didn't matter. If he was going to do the right thing, if he was going to make his sacrifice and all that his grandfather had sacrificed worth it, he had to keep moving forward.

We just have to do the best we can. Be smarter and better than them.

Blood was running down his face now, being washed out of his hair by the pounding rain. He could barely see where he was going, but that wouldn't stop his descent into the gray valley below, or whatever it might turn into between here and there. Maybe he would fail, but it wouldn't be because he gave up. Wiping his face, he started forward again, his expression grim and resolved.

I'm trying, Grandpa. And I won't stop.

Time means little when traveling in the Nightlands, particularly when it comes to day and night. He walked for what felt like a day or more by his internal clock, never growing hungry or thirsty or stopping for more than a few moments here or there, and he had seen things shift around him more than a dozen times, including several periods of day and night. The transitions were always jarring, but he did find himself getting...well, not used to them, but less bothered by them. And while he worried that he might be the one that was jumping around and not the land itself, his strange instinct said that wasn't so, and that he was still making progress on his path toward...something.

Twice so far he'd seen what looked like the distant shapes of large villages, and both times he'd almost stopped. One of the key things he needed was information—had anyone run across something like the Gravekeeper? Had he actually beaten it to the Nightlands, and if so, by how much? For all he knew, Emily may not have been able to place him at a different point in time at all, but only a different place. Or worse yet, between her abilities and the way time worked in the Nightlands, he could be arriving well after the Gravekeeper had already accomplished whatever terrible goals it had in this Realm.

But he wasn't being pulled that way, was he?

In his short time in the Nightlands, he'd come to rely and trust his new instincts a lot more than he had before. It was a risk, as there was always the possibility that the Outsider influence that had fundamentally changed him was also working on his mind. Manipulating him into a trap of some sort. Still, he didn't think so, and given his options, he couldn't see turning away the only guidance he had. So he kept walking, holding out hope that when he was meant to find someone, his path and theirs would naturally meet.

It so happened that meeting came sooner rather than later.

When Jason heard the cry for help, it wasn't in words he could understand or even words at all. It was a wild, inarticulate cry of terror and despair that needed no further nuance or subtle detail. Because it was clear that it was the sound of a creature that was about to die.

He pivoted at the sound, discarding any pretense of precaution as he went from a fast walk to a jolting sprint, each step growing faster and longer of stride as he dove into the midnight woods to his right in the direction of the scream. He had no idea what he was headed toward, but he knew he had to try and help. That scream had not been unintelligent—it was pregnant with fear and dread for its owner's doom.

Seeing a dim flicker of firelight between the trees ahead, Jason leapt forward into a clearing. Down on the ground before him, the size of a small adult or a large child, was something that looked like a fox, though its hands were articulate enough for it to hold a small wooden torch up as though to ward him off. Again he felt the flush of how bizarre everything was here, and again he pushed it aside. He looked around for anyone else, either an attacker or a victim, but there was neither. Given how terrified this creature looked, he doubted it was a trap. But how could he...

"Please, run. It'll just kill you too."

The fox had just talked. Jason blinked, it taking a moment for the import of its words to sink in. When they did, he looked around the clearing warily. "What is it? What's trying to kill you?" Swallowing, he looked back at the creature. "Is it a man? One that looks as though he's rotting away?"

The fox showed mild surprise through its terror. "A man? No, it's a drovik. They usually don't leave their caves, but..." It shook it's head. "It's already marked me. It won't stop hunting me. But you can still get away maybe." It gave a little shooing gesture with its free hand. "Go, go now."

He scanned the area around them, listening carefully for any sound from their surroundings or for any whispers from his internal guide. Both were equally silent.

"I know you don't see it. It can turn invisible, and despite its size, it can climb trees easily. It's hiding up there somewhere right now. It crawled up when it heard you coming." The creature's voice trembled slightly. "It's watching us."

Jason listened to what the fox said, but he had no intention of leaving him behind. He could pick him up, run back out of the woods, and if the creature that had been hunting him followed, at least he could fight it away from these tall, dark trees. The key was just to…

A spray of yellow flew out of the darkness, hitting him low on the right shoulder. He felt his arm immediately begin to go numb. Looking around, he saw the branches of a nearby tree bowing under the weight of some unseen thing. Behind him, the fox let out a moan.

"Oh no! He's marked you…I'm sorry. I'm sorry…"

The tree's bough flexed down and Jason jumped back just before something landed in the spot where he'd been. This close, he could see the shimmering outline of something massive and terrible in the meager torchlight, and the next moment he could see more than he wanted as the drovik revealed itself.

Ten feet tall and twelve feet wide, it had a barrel-chested body and eight muscular legs covered in brown spotted fur. Those legs ended in hook-like claws that it scraped across the ground regularly as it regarded Jason, reminding him of a bull getting ready to charge. Malice burned out of its broad skull from three eyes of blazing blue, with a fourth eye on the far right milky and dead from some past injury. At first, it reminded Jason of some nightmare mix between a bear and a spider.

But then its head split open.

It opened in four directions at once, spreading out like a hideous blossom filled with gray meat, black teeth, and questing tongues of scarlet. Jason took another step back, weighing his chances of grabbing the fox creature and making a run for it. He could sense it was about to attack, and it was already making some kind of growl or...No, it wasn't growling.

It was laughing.

In that moment, Jason thought back to sitting in his parents' kitchen as his grandfather told him about chasing Marcus Salk after he'd abducted that little boy. About running through the woods, trying to reach him in time. About seeing Salk's monstrous other form and trying to shoot it, stop it. About how it had laughed at him as it killed the boy.

Suddenly, all Jason's fear and doubt were gone, replaced with a stronger and purer form of the anger and need to kill he'd been feeling ever since his change. This thing wanted to kill them both, and if this fox was right, it wouldn't stop until it did. And then it'd find someone else and do it again. Because that's what it was—a hunter, a killer, a monster.

That was all right. So was he.

Surging forward, he grasped the top corners of its mouth before it could react. He yanked hard in both directions, and he saw rivulets of dark blood forming at the fissures in its flesh even as it yet out an angry yell and tried to pull away. His left hand held its grip, but his right was weaker from whatever it had sprayed on his shoulder, and he lost his purchase even as it swiped a claw across his middle, disemboweling him.

Grunting, Jason curled his right hand into a fist and sent it arcing into the side of the thing's head with a crack that caused it to stumble. He could already feel his stomach healing itself, but this thing was too strong and too unknown to let up for a moment. He sent a second and third punch into its head, and on the fourth he felt the skull begin to give way.

That's when the drovik rolled. With a lightness and grace he would have thought impossible given its size, it rolled onto its back. And because Jason was still holding onto its mouth with his left hand, he was carried over into its waiting legs.

It started tearing him apart immediately, and he had no doubt that for most things this would work exceedingly well at ending the fight. Unfortunately for it, as savage and damaging as its attacks were, he could heal faster, and as determined as it was to pull him down away from its head, he just wouldn't let go.

Jason didn't know what other tricks this thing might have, and he didn't have long before it figured out this one wasn't working. He needed to end this now. The drovik had been primarily ripping apart his back, which had the side benefit of tearing away most of the numbing slime it had sprayed him with in the process. Pulling himself up slightly for a better angle, he used his right hand to start ripping out the thing's throat. He had to time his blows for when he was healed enough at any given moment, but by the time it realized what he was doing, it was too late. After a few seconds he had ripped away a black, stony mass that he supposed passed for its spine and sent its massive head rolling to the foot of a nearby tree.

He lay on the thing's furry chest for a moment to catch his breath. He was feeling strangely winded at the moment, and his hand was burning and going numb again at the same time. Jason looked at it and saw it was covered in not only blood, but some lighter, pinkish liquid as well. Poison? Rolling off the creature, he wiped his hand frantically on the ground. Shit, got overconfident and now I've fucked up. I need to get this off...

Jason felt the world closing in on him, as though every sight and sound was coming to him through a tiny pinhole in the dark world that was enveloping him. The last thing he saw was two large padded feet walking to him as everything fell away.

"Asha, get away from him."

"I was just looking, Papa."

"I know what you were doing, knurlcaff. But our friend is sick. Leave him be."

Jason tried to move his eyes, and at first, it was impossible. He heard more sounds around him, and he found himself wondering if he was coming out of a dream or going into one. He could smell something cooking, and for the first time since coming to the Nightlands, he realized he was hungry. Spurred on by this hunger, he pushed harder against the bounds of the darkness that held him, and after a struggle, he cracked his eyes open.

He was inside. In a house of some sort. He thought he was laying either on the floor or a low bed, but if so, the ceiling of swirling wood between patches of color seemed oddly low. Turning his head with an effort, he saw the fox he had saved sitting nearby in a chair.

"Hello, my friend. It is good to see you awake again. You've been asleep for two days, and I worried the drovik's poison might never let you go." It raised its dark eyebrows and let out a chuckle. "Though to be fair, most would have been dead within moments of touching that foul venom. So all things considered, a bit of sleep seems like a fair trade."

His mouth was dry and unwieldy, but when he tried, he found he could talk with only a mild slur. "Is this...your home?"

The fox nodded, his face seeming to brighten with pride. "Yes, mine and my family's. I came and got help from our city to bring you here to rest."

Jason nodded. "Thank...thank you."

The fox chuckled again. "Not at all. You

saved my life. There was nothing else I *could* do."

He had an important question somewhere in his mind. What was it..."When is it?...I mean, what year is it?"

The creature studied him for a moment. "I thought you must not be from here. Where do you come from? The terrestrial Realm?"

Jason went to ask what he meant, but then he felt that little tug in the back of his mind. "Yes. I'm from that Realm." Thinking, he added. "Do you have any idea what the date is...the day and month and year...in that Realm?"

The fox furrowed his brow for a moment. "Not exactly, no. We live in a place that is very steady...it doesn't change often and time keeps its pace. But it is still the Nightlands." Looking at Jason's expression, he tapped a black nail to his chin. "But based on what I heard last, I'd guess the year there was...around 1150 or so?"

Sitting up suddenly, his head began to swim so violently that he had to lay back down. "1150? Like the year 1150?"

The creature shrugged its small shoulders. "Yes, I think so. Give or take a decade or two. 1150 A.D., I think you call it." He reached out and patted Jason's shoulder with a furry hand. "I can tell this upsets you, but try not to let it. Most things we can sort out. Most that we can't, still get sorted in the end. You need to rest now."

Jason wanted to protest, but he could already feel sleep pressing him back down. Maybe this was all just a dream after all. How could it not be? Wait, the fox was asking another question. "What..what was that?"

The fox patted his shoulder again and chuckled. "I just asked your name. If you trust me enough to give it, of course."

Nodding, he replied. "Yeah...Yeah I do...It's Jason." Even in his sleepiness, he weighed his next words for a moment. This was the first person he had met, perhaps the first friend he had made, in this magical new world. Who was he going to be here? It didn't take long for him to realize he already knew the answer. "My name is Jason Barron."

"A pleasure to meet you. Now get some more sleep. Supper will be ready when you wake."

Jason began to drift back to sleep, but as he did so, he heard soft footfalls approaching from the other side of the bed.

"Asha, I said leave him be."

"I am, Papa. I just wanted to see him closer. Reve and Tori will never believe it when I tell them."

"Tell them what, Asha? You're making no sense."

"That we've got a monster slayer staying with us. Who killed a drovik with his bare hands!"

Another low chuckle. "And not only that, kit. Make sure to tell them the rest." He was fading fast now, but he struggled to hold on and hear more.

"What's that, Papa?"

"Why that he's also royalty. I just heard it from him myself. Let them all know that our guest...our heroic, monster-slaying guest...is also a Baron."

Made in the USA
Las Vegas, NV
05 May 2023